Glass King

Midnight Empire: The Restoration, Book 3

Annabel Chase

Red Palm Press LLC

Cover by trifbookdesign.com

Created with Vellum

Chapter One

Lava glowed like red-orange tentacles in the deepest, darkest corner of the ocean. The intense heat threatened to melt my skin off the bones. A single, panicked thought flashed in my mind.

Please don't be another Great Eruption.

Ten of the world's supervolcanoes erupting at the same time was quite enough of a show for one planet. No need for an encore. Then again, the sun was already blocked thanks to the density of the debris in the atmosphere. What harm could another eruption do?

I looked at the landscape of magma and ash and pictured all the monsters that had climbed from the earth's core during that fateful time.

Never mind.

Above me a lone bird flew overheard with its black and white wings spread wide. A large vulture of some kind, likely waiting to see if I'd succumb to my surroundings and provide the bird with much-needed sustenance. I couldn't imagine the carrion-eater had much luck in this desolate place.

Lava continued to drain from the mouth of the volcano. If I wasn't careful, the lava would claim me the way it had claimed everything else in its path.

In the darkness a speck of green and gold caught my eye.

A butterfly—here?

Despite the comforting sight of those familiar colors, I knew the butterfly wasn't Alaric. The king was safe in his New York compound, while I was...not.

The wings of the butterfly beckoned me. I drew a deep breath and started toward it. I never thought I'd view a butterfly as a beacon of hope, yet here I was, following its lead—hopefully to safety.

My foot slipped on a slick rock and I tumbled to the ground. Steam burst from the earth and I rolled to the side before it could scald me.

"Britt," the butterfly said. "Get up."

A female voice. So familiar.

I crawled across the rocks on my stomach, unable to stand.

"Come on, Britt."

I peered ahead but could no longer see the butterfly.

"Britt, I need you!"

The urgency in her voice jolted me and I bolted upright. A cool, damp cloth slipped from my forehead onto my lap.

"Thank the gods." A woman gazed at me with joyous relief. With black hair that spilled across her shoulders like pools of ink and sharp gray eyes, she seemed vaguely familiar, but I couldn't place her.

My throat felt dry and slightly swollen. "I'm sick?"

She nodded. "Three days."

I glanced around the cramped space. It was no larger

than five feet by eight feet with a low, domed ceiling. Some kind of hut. The furnishings were basically nonexistent, and the wooden flooring was partially covered by a hand-braided blue and ivory rug. There was another bedroll aside from mine. No actual beds. I spotted a separate sink and toilet but no shower or tub. Nowhere to hide.

"Where am I?"

"Lancaster County. You don't remember?" Her brow creased. "Do you know your name?"

"Britt." No last name. I'd ditched Miller years ago. It was the surname of my parents and I had no use for it.

"Do you know my name?" she asked.

I studied her face. Memories pushed their way forward. A god trapped in a book. Rivers to oblivion.

Then I remembered.

"London Hayes." Knight of Boudica. Witch. She'd come to my aid in New York and was repaid for her kindness with a kidnapping to my hometown. "I'm so sorry. This is all my fault."

A relieved smile touched her lips. "Not at all. I'm glad you're awake. I've been worried about you."

"I'm better now, I think."

She brought a cup of water to my chapped mouth. "You should drink. I've been trying to keep you hydrated, but you've been unconscious much of the time."

"Thank you." I took a grateful sip. "Do you think someone will check on us soon?"

London shrugged. "No idea. They don't come like clockwork, which I'm sure is a deliberate tactic."

I drew my knees to my chest and tried to reorient myself.

"They're doing the bare minimum," London explained. "They want us alive but not necessarily comfortable."

I noticed cuts on both our palms. "Did they cut our hands?"

"No, we did. We tried to use our blood to break the ward. Needless to say, it didn't work." She offered a weak smile. "And they took our forks away after that."

A harsh whisper escaped me. "Olis."

The wizard had betrayed me.

I rested my chin in the dip between my knees. The Director of Security for House August had pretended to be an ally. He had promised to support and defend King Alaric.

All lies.

"He drugged us during our celebratory drink," London reminded me. "We woke up here."

More memories stirred. "This place is warded," I said.

London nodded. "To the max. They planned for this. Neither one of us can use magic in here."

No weapons. No magic. Even with London and I at full health, the Lancaster coven had the upper hand. I wondered whether everyone in the coven was a member of Trinity Group or whether they'd simply struck a deal. Not that it made any difference from my point of view.

I drank more water to quench my thirst. Every sip seemed to restore my strength.

"Remind me what kind of magic you can do," I said. Although the knight and I had worked together to deliver the soul of a god for judgment, I was fairly sure I hadn't witnessed every tool in her magical arsenal.

Hesitation flickered in her gray eyes. "What does it matter?"

She seemed uncertain of me, which surprised me. I thought we'd bonded during our adventure in Central Park.

"I'm trying to assess our escape options once we break free of this prison."

"Believe me, I've been running through a dozen scenarios, but all of them required you to be conscious."

"Which I now am." I tried to offer a reassuring smile, but it probably looked more like a grimace.

"Don't tax yourself," she advised. "I need you at full capacity if we expect to leave here in one piece."

I snapped my fingers, remembering. "You can open portals." That was a rare and sought-after skill.

"Yes. I can also communicate with animals."

"That'll come in handy when we want to play fetch."

She smiled. "I try to win them over to my side."

I frowned. "Win them over?"

"I don't control them per se, but I...encourage them to do my bidding."

At the mention of animals, my thoughts turned to George, my beloved companion. Poor George would be worried sick about me. I pictured the phoenix desperately trying to explain my absence to those who couldn't understand him. Surely Liam would see George and realize something horrible must've happened to me. I would never leave him behind.

London loomed over me with motherly concern. "Are you feeling unwell again?"

"No, I'm worried about my friends." Olis was too clever to leave those stones unturned. The wizard knew Liam and George were liabilities. There was no telling what he might've done to keep them quiet about my absence.

"You think Olis might've hurt them?"

I nodded. "At the very least, he sidelined them. It would buy him time so Alaric would believe I left the city as I originally planned. One sighting of George and the king would know something was wrong."

"I would like to think Callan is searching for me, but there's every chance Olis managed to cover my tracks, too."

"King Callan wouldn't consider it strange for you to be out of touch?"

She offered a rueful smile. "The downside of being an independent woman. It isn't unusual at all, especially if I'm working on a mission."

"But your mission is over and the Knights of Boudica and Princess Davina will have returned to Britannia City without you."

London took the damp cloth from my lap and tossed it into the sink. "He may grow concerned, but it may not happen as soon as we need."

And he'd never in a million years think to look for his beloved in Lancaster, North America.

"What about you?" London asked, returning to sit on her bedroll beside mine. "Blood magic, right?"

"That's pretty much it in terms of magic."

"A rare skill, though."

"Like yours." A thought occurred to me. "When I met with members of Trinity Group, they mentioned a mind, body, and spirit in connection with the prophecy. That's where they took their name, I think."

London rolled her eyes. "If I never hear about this bloody prophecy again, it'll be too soon."

The prophecy was, of course, the reason we were here. Trinity Group believed that London and I were instrumental to a plan to bring back the sun and overthrow vampire rule.

"Let me guess," London continued. "You're the body."

I nodded. "You must be the mind."

London plucked a loose thread on the bedroll. "Seems unfair. Kami's the one with mind control powers, not that I'd want her to trade places with me." Her voice dropped. "She's my best friend. I wouldn't wish this on her, or even Minka for that matter."

"Minka's an enemy?"

"Oh, no. She's a friend, albeit a very annoying one."

I smiled. "I wonder why they've decided you're the other witch in the prophecy."

There it was, that flash of hesitation again. London knew—or at least suspected—something, but whatever it was, she wasn't sharing. I thought I could trust her, but maybe that trust was misplaced. Wouldn't be the first time.

London changed the subject. "What can you tell me about our captors? So far, I've only met three adult witches, a wizard, and two girls. The girls seem to be here for observational purposes."

I sipped more water. "The coven believes in hands-on learning." Although I didn't recall 'How to Care for Captives' as part of my early education. "They probably haven't said much when they come in. They like their secrets." And excelled at keeping them.

London lowered her gaze to the floor. "While we're on the subject of secrets, there's something you should know about me. Something that might help us."

"I'm all ears."

She looked at me. "I'm technically a princess."

I laughed. "How can you be a princess? You're a witch."

"Not quite." London held up her left hand. "Vampire king." She raised her right hand. "Witch." She slammed her hands together. "Me."

"That's very good. If we live through this, you should consider becoming a teacher like your mother." My brain shrieked in protest as her demonstration sank in. "Wait a hot minute. Your father..."

London eyed me carefully. "Yes?"

"You're a dhampir," I whispered.

"Congratulations. You've aced this mini biology quiz."

I gawked at her. "I've never met..."

She performed a mock bow from her seated position. "Living abomination at your service, madam."

"Hey, me too!" We fist bumped and I realized *this* was the secret she'd been reluctant to tell me. The fact that she was willing to confide in me now was significant.

London trusted me.

"How is this helpful, though?" I asked. "I don't think the coven cares about your royal blood."

"That's not the relevant part." She dropped her voice to a whisper. "It means I can do more than magic."

My mind raced through the possibilities. Vampires possessed speed, strength, agility...I stared at her. "You can turn invisible."

Vampire characteristics weren't magical; therefore, the ward wouldn't account for them.

"It isn't a surefire way out of here," London said, "but it's better than nothing. Only I wasn't willing to make a move without you."

I liked to think I would've done the same in her position, although I wasn't accustomed to working with a team the way she was.

The creak of the door interrupted us, and we turned to watch a portly witch push her way into the room. Behind her, a younger witch carried a tray with two bowls and spoons.

The older witch stopped short at the sight of me.

"You've improved." She didn't sound particularly pleased about the development.

"Hello, Francesca."

She glowered at me. "Don't dare speak to me as if you know me."

"But I do know you. You pulled me by the ear all the way to my parents when you learned what I could do." It was hard to forget the woman who first discovered my particular brand of magic and was quick to condemn it as 'dirty' and 'the devil's handiwork.' I'd spent years shooting targets while imagining Francesca's face on them. Sometimes I wondered whether the coven would've reacted so harshly if Francesca hadn't set the tone upon her discovery. If my parents wouldn't have been so quick to share my secret and allow the coven to shun me.

The young witch lowered the tray to the floor and stepped back with her head bowed.

"Thank you. What's your name?" I asked. With her brown hair parted in the middle and styled in two braids, she looked no older than ten.

"Don't answer that," Francesca snapped. "You don't speak to the prisoners."

"I prefer the term 'honored guests,'" I said. "How's your earth magic coming along, Franny? If I recall correctly, you were once able to help the coven grow a whole rosebush." Francesca's earth magic had been weak, and she'd been relegated to what the coven sometimes referred to as 'the chorus.' No solos for Francesca. Even as a child, I could tell her limited magic irked her to no end, which was probably the reason she was so angry when she discovered my rare type of magic.

Francesca glared at me. "Rose petals are extremely important to the coven."

"Oh, I'm sure. Without them, you might smell like lavender instead."

The young witch stifled a giggle. Francesca's face grew flush with rage, and she smacked the back of the girl's head. "Show some respect, you insolent brat."

London jumped to her full height. "Whoa, pick on someone your own size. You can start with me."

"I'm afraid you're off limits, which is too bad," Francesca said with a sniff. "I would be more than happy to start with you."

I sighed at London. "Score another one for the prophecy, I guess."

"Not to worry. Your day will come and I, for one, cannot wait to watch you burn." Francesca cackled with unbridled glee.

The door opened again and another witch joined our party. Her nose sported a small bump, and her brown hair was worn long and loose around her shoulders.

"Valentina," I blurted.

The witch met my gaze. "You remember me?"

"Of course." Valentina was in charge of the root vegetables. Another witch with earth magic, slightly more powerful than Francesca.

Francesca turned to scold the late arrival. "Stop speaking to her as if she's one of us. She's no better than the monsters born during the Great Eruption."

Valentina's face grew pinched. "Shush, Fran. There's no need..."

"No need?" Francesca interrupted her. "Have you forgotten what she is? What she's done? There's every need." The vengeful witch waved a hand at us. "They both consort with the Fallen." She spared us a glance. "Which is why we made sure to scrub you both clean of any diseases you might've brought with you. We can't afford an outbreak in our little community."

The Lancaster coven viewed the entire vampire species as a plague from another realm that spread death and disease and looked at other advanced species simply as sources of food and nothing more. The worst offense, of course, was that the Fallen prohibited magic except in service of a House, which resulted in the suppression of generations of witches and wizards.

"You obviously didn't scrub me clean enough if I managed to fall ill for three days."

Francesca sauntered closer to me. "That may have been the result of something I slipped into your food. You and your disgusting friend will pay for your misguided allegiances. Just you wait until the ritual."

"I'm sure it's a lovely custom that involves unicorns and rainbows," London said.

Francesca bent over until her face was only an inch from mine. "You'll be tied to the stake, your hearts cut out with the Blade of Fire, the blood drained from your bodies, and then the pièce de résistance. You will burn with the heat of a thousand suns. The smoke from your pyre will rise up to the heavens and tear apart the dark blanket that smothers us. And the sun's rays will bathe us in light once more, courtesy of your charred corpses." She punctuated her description with a chef's kiss.

I looked at London. "All I heard was witches burning other witches at the stake."

"That's what I heard, too," she confirmed.

I turned back to Francesca. "You don't see the irony in that?"

Francesca reared up. "I don't care. Whatever it takes to

rid this world of vampires. If your death is required in the process, I consider that a bonus."

"She *really* doesn't like you," London observed.

"The feeling is mutual."

Francesca smacked my face. My cheek stung but I managed to maintain a neutral expression. No way was she getting a rise out of me.

"Sounds like you need a hobby," I told her calmly. "Or maybe the skilled hands of a lover."

Valentina grabbed Francesca's wrist before she could slap me again. "Enough, Fran. Let's go."

Francesca stormed out of the hut, leaving Valentina and the young witch behind.

"I'm sorry about that," Valentina said, once the door slammed shut. "She's been harboring ill will for a very long time because of..." She couldn't bring herself to say the words.

"Because of what happened at the market," I finished for her. I'd been in Philadelphia for a job and spotted two witches at the market that I knew from Lancaster. They'd been horrible to me before my exile. One had even spit on me for possessing 'dirty magic.' I was seven years old at the time. The second I saw them at the market, that moment came rushing back to me and I snapped. I nearly killed them right there in the market.

Francesca was one of them.

Valentina's head snapped to attention. "You regret your actions?"

I nodded. "Very much." And I'd paid for them, too, as an indentured servant for House August.

Valentina dipped her head slightly. "I appreciate you saying so. I'm sure Francesca would, too."

Fat chance.

"What more can you tell us about the prophecy?" I asked. I thought if I could keep her comfortable and talking, she might reveal something we could use to aid in our escape.

Valentina's eyes flickered with uncertainty. "How much do you know?"

I latched on to what Francesca revealed during her tirade. "You need to sacrifice us with a special dagger." I paused. "The Dagger of Flames or something."

"The Blade of Fire," Valentina corrected me.

I offered a disinterested shrug. "Never heard of it."

"I haven't heard of it either," London said, "and my mother was a history teacher."

"To be honest, I'm not convinced it exists. Sounds more like an Excalibur-type story," Valentina said.

I resisted looking at London. "Then you don't have the dagger?"

Valentina shook her head. "From what I've heard, Trinity Group has had teams looking for ages, but nobody's found it yet."

"And what about the third witch?" I asked. "Olis said you had teams searching for her, too. Any luck?"

"Not yet. As you can imagine, it isn't easy to scour the earth for a single pebble." She offered a wry smile.

"What makes you so certain this third witch exists?" London asked.

"The prophecy has been confirmed by multiple sources," Valentina told us.

"But prophecies aren't written in stone," I countered. "They're more like suggestions to the universe."

"You cannot fight fate, Britt the Bloody," Valentina said with a degree of sympathy. "The prophecy has been foretold and it *will* come to pass—one way or another." She hesitated. "But for what it's worth, I would rather not sacrifice either of you in order to bring it forth. Doesn't seem right."

"But you're willing to stand by and let them do it," I said. "That makes you complicit."

Her face fell. "I'm not proud of it."

"Neither am I," the young witch chimed in. "I think it's a travesty."

"Now, now," Valentina said. "Let's not be disrespectful."

"Why not? We're being disrespectful to *them*." She nodded at us.

"We've explained their importance to you already," Valentina said with an impressive measure of calm. Francesca would've bashed the girl in the head by now. "Without the sacrifice, the vampires will continue to rule over us."

"Then we should let them," the girl said. "If we're willing to kill our own kind to be in charge, maybe we don't deserve it."

"Well said," London told her.

Valentina pursed her lips. "It isn't that I disagree. I've always maintained there ought to be a way of meeting in the middle, but I've been outvoted every time. I even voted against your removal back when..." She trailed off. "It doesn't matter now. I'm not the head of the coven and I never will be." She motioned to the tray. "Eat up. Every day there's another witch arguing against feeding you. I worry one day soon they'll get their way."

My gaze drifted to the bowl of soup. "Vegetable?"

"For this one here." Valentina nodded to London. "She doesn't eat meat, not that we have a lot of that to go around anyway."

"Thank you," London said. "Your kindness is appreciated."

Valentina seemed mildly embarrassed by London's show of gratitude.

An impatient knock on the door interrupted us. "Is everything all right in there?"

Valentina rolled her eyes. "Yes, Kathleen."

The young witch stiffened at the name. She shot Valentina a pleading look.

"Who's in there with you?" Kathleen demanded.

I remembered Kathleen. She and Francesca had been cut from the same cloth. No tolerance for children and definitely no tolerance for anyone 'different.'

"None of your concern," Valentina called back. She smoothed the young witch's hair. "Come on then. I'm sure you're wanted at the aviary."

The young witch seemed rooted in place. Finally, she tore herself from where she stood and advanced toward the door.

"Talia," she whispered as she passed us. "My name is Talia."

Chapter Two

My dreams were as fraught with danger and terror as the last time. Another sleep, another visit to a fiery caldera. It seemed my sickness had little to do with the content.

London nudged me awake. "I'm glad I don't have your nightmares. Do I even want to know what's happening in your head?"

I rubbed my temples. "I'm not sure I could tell you. They remind me of nightmares I had as a kid."

"It's probably the fact that you're back in Lancaster."

"Could be." I drew myself into a seated position. "My father used to scold me for crying out in my sleep." And so I learned to muffle my terrified sobs.

"Did you continue to have them once you left the coven?"

"Once or twice." The caldera nightmares were then replaced by more pressing terrors. Homelessness. Starvation. Violence. If not for the generosity of those I met on the road, I'd have died long ago.

"How many members of the coven do you remember?" London asked.

"Most of the adults we've seen." Not that we'd seen very many. They were careful to avoid us. I had to imagine they were afraid, despite their precautions. I couldn't say I blamed them.

"Is there anybody here who might break ranks? Valentina seemed to have a soft spot."

"Doubtful. The coven is a well-oiled machine when it comes to following orders and fulfilling your duties."

"Sounds a lot like a House."

"They're not as dissimilar as they like to believe." They could be as wonderful as each other and equally as terrible.

"I'd throw packs in there, too," London said.

"I haven't known any packs well enough to comment. Only lone wolves." Which was probably not a coincidence.

"I keep waiting for my skin to glow," London said. "When my magic is suppressed too long, I turn silver. The buildup can get unbearable."

"But that isn't happening?"

She shook her head. "It must be the ward."

"I have no doubt they've done their homework on us and poured everything they have into this prison. We're too important to them to only go halfway."

I heard the lock turn. The door flew open and Francesca appeared in the doorway. She looked as unhappy to see me as I felt about seeing her.

"How did you end up drawing the lucky straw again?" I asked.

"It's time to wash in the sink." Francesca tossed a bar of soap into the water. "And here's a towel to dry yourself after."

"Only one?" I asked. "There are two of us."

"You can share."

"I had better service alone in the middle of the forest," I grumbled.

"You're lucky to be getting soap. If I had it my way..."

"We know, we know," I said. "We'd be dead already."

"Well, I'd starve you first. You don't deserve mercy."

A busty woman muscled her way past Francesca. Kathleen.

"A shame," Kathleen said, assessing me. "You look like both of them."

By 'them,' I realized she meant my parents. "You came in here just to tell me that?"

"No, I came in because no one is supposed to be here alone." She shot a pointed look at Francesca. "There's no telling what the two of you are capable of. If I'd had my way, you'd be in two separate huts."

"Why aren't we?" I asked.

"Because it would be a drain on resources. Plus, nobody wanted to give up their space. This one's been spare since Gunther died."

Gunther Abbott. I remembered the old, kindly wizard. He'd be appalled to learn his home was being used as a prison. Gunther had been one of the few good ones.

"How long do you intend to keep us here?" London demanded.

"As long as it takes to perform the ritual," Kathleen replied.

"That could take years," I shot back.

The witch shrugged. "If that's how long it takes."

"Where's Olis? Will he visit or is he too afraid to show his face?"

"Olis Tuttle is otherwise engaged." The smirk on the witch's face gave me pause.

"Engaged with what? I thought we were the most important task."

"You are only part of a plan," Francesca said. "Although it doesn't surprise me that you'd think you were the most critical piece. You always were an arrogant little witch."

Unease spread through my limbs. Olis worked for House August. If he was part of another plan, it had to involve Alaric.

"I'd like to see my parents," I announced. I'd waited at first, thinking they'd come of their accord, but maybe the coven had restricted visitation.

Our captors exchanged looks. "Your parents are dead," Francesca said without a trace of remorse.

"They were very fine members of the coven," Kathleen added. "They are sorely missed."

"What happened to them?"

"We had an outbreak a few years ago, after a couple wizards returned from a supply trip," Kathleen explained. "We lost a dozen members, your parents among them."

I waited to feel something—anything—but I didn't.

"Your sister survived, so your line hasn't been completely lost," Kathleen continued.

I thought I might've misheard her. "I'm sorry. Did you say my sister?"

Francesca was only too happy to tell me more. "You wouldn't know, would you? She was born after you were cast out. I believe your parents wanted to replace you, to prove they were capable of creating more than a monster." She practically spat the words at me.

My heart beat rapidly as I absorbed the news. "Does she know I'm here?"

"She knows we have two monsters on lockdown and that's all she needs to know." Francesca picked up an empty tray from the floor. "Let's go, Kathleen. It makes my skin crawl to breathe the same air as them."

They turned and left.

"They're real charmers," London said. "Were they this nice to you when you lived here?"

"Everybody was nice until they discovered a reason not to be."

The door opened a crack and a small hand appeared clutching a towel. The hand released the towel and quickly withdrew.

London and I exchanged smiles. It seemed the young witch had decided to rebel in her own way. A kindred spirit.

"Do you know my sister?" I whispered through the crack.

"Yes," came the soft reply.

"What's her name?"

"Saffron."

"Does she know who I am?"

"No."

Didn't think so. "Can you bring her to me so I can talk to her?"

Silence.

"Listen, Talia, wouldn't you want to know if you had an older sister out there, especially if your parents were dead? I'm the only family she has."

"She has the coven," the young witch replied.

"Ah, yes. The coven. You can see how well that's worked out for some of us. Could be you, too, if you put a foot wrong." I felt her continued presence on the other side of the door, which was a good sign. I kept talking. "I know a place where children live in harmony. No parents. Brothers and sisters look after each other. Humans, mostly, but maybe I could take her there. Protect her."

A long pause and then—

"All right. I'll bring her to you."

I closed my eyes and breathed a sigh of relief. "Thank you."

"Do you think she'll care?" London asked, once Talia had gone. "There's a good chance they've indoctrinated her."

"There is, but there's also a chance she has a little spark of me in her." I shrugged. "I'd like to see."

"How old do you think she is?"

I smiled. "Let's hope it's the ripe old age of rebellion."

Hours later Saffron Miller appeared in our prison. She shut the door quickly behind her, keeping her back flat against it. "Talia said you wanted to see me."

I was unprepared for my reaction. She shared my blond hair and athletic build, although she was an inch taller. She still had that hint of awkwardness that marked her as a teenager.

"You're Saffron Miller?"

"Why do you care?"

"My name is Britt."

"I know who you are, Britt the Bloody. We're not supposed to speak to either of you. The coven says you're dangerous."

"Then why did you come?"

She fidgeted with the fabric of her skirt. "I wanted to see for myself."

I drew closer to her. "What do you see, Saffron?"

Her gaze darted to London and back to me. "Two witches like me. You don't seem very dangerous."

"What's your magic?"

"Elemental, but my strength is air."

Like our mother. "Do I look familiar to you at all?"

She peered at my face. "Should you?"

"Did anyone tell you who I am?"

"You're the blood witch. Part of a prophecy to bring back the sun."

"My name was Britt Miller when I lived here as a little girl, before they cast me out."

Saffron blinked at me. "Cousin?"

"Sister."

She scowled as she recoiled. "You're lying."

"Why would I lie about a thing like that?"

"You're trying to manipulate me."

"If I wanted to manipulate someone, it would be the little girl who brought you here. Look at me, Saffron. We have our mother's hair color. The shape of our father's eyes."

"Impossible. You're a blood witch. We don't have any filthy magic in our family."

I spread my arms wide. "Consider me your dirty little secret."

Her lips parted. "Why wouldn't they have told me?"

"Because they were ashamed." Ashamed of me. And ashamed of what they did to me. "They cast me out when I was a little girl and left me to die."

Anger sparked in her eyes. "They would never!"

"But they did. I was only seven. Younger than Talia. I survived thanks to the kindness of strangers."

"And your own grit," London added. "Don't forget to give yourself some credit." I was so focused on my sister, I'd almost forgotten she was there.

Saffron folded her arms. "What do you want from me?"

"Isn't it obvious? I want you to help us escape."

She barked a laugh. "You're insane if you think I'd turn on the coven."

"Why not? They'd turn on you in a heartbeat if it suited them."

"Well, it wouldn't suit them. I'm an elemental witch. They need me."

"And they need me more but look how they're treating me." I motioned to the cramped prison. "They're planning to sacrifice us, you know that, right?"

Her mouth formed a thin line. She knew.

"Our parents are dead and now you've learned your sister is alive. Are you really going to let them kill me?"

"It's for the greater good," she said, her chin sliding upward in the direction of righteousness. "If it were me, I'd be willing to sacrifice myself to free us from vampire oppression."

Easier said than done. "There's no guarantee it will work."

"And there's no guarantee it's the only way to achieve your goal," London chimed in. "Prophecies are finicky and not always accurate. Do you really want your sister's blood on your hands?"

Saffron seemed to waver. "I can't let you go. They'll know it was me."

"Not necessarily. We can make it seem like we overpowered you. That you tried to fight back."

"They'll still blame me. I'll be shunned. They'll cancel the wedding."

I balked. "Wedding? You're old enough to get married?"

"I'm seventeen. They need more witches and wizards for the cause. The sooner we wed and give birth, the better."

"Better for whom?" I asked. "Saffron, did you even choose this guy?"

Her head drooped. Great gods above, they were turning the coven into a baby factory to create a magical army.

"Saffron, you have your whole life ahead of you," I said. "You don't have to listen to them. You can leave. Live the life that you want."

"Like you did?" she asked with a bitter laugh.

"I was cast out," I said, "but at least I wasn't forced to be a teen bride."

"Maybe you should've been. Then maybe you wouldn't have tried to murder everybody in that market."

I opened mouth to respond but no words came out.

Her eyebrows lifted. "See? I know what kind of monster you are and there's no way I'm letting you out of here." She inched toward the exit.

"We're family, Saffron."

"We're nothing," she said, and rapped on the door. An unseen hand opened the door from the outside and Saffron slipped through the gap without another word.

Once the door closed, I spun to face London. "A rousing success, wouldn't you say?"

"You took her by surprise. Give her time to process."

I jabbed my thumb over my shoulder. "We were witness to the same conversation, right? No way is that witch going to help us."

"You never know. She might mellow given time..."

"There is no time," I shot back. "We need to get out of here and quickly."

"I'm open to suggestions."

I sighed. "It's time to put your dhampir side to work."

She cast her gaze at the window. "How far do you think the ward extends?"

I considered the question. "I suspect there are layers. This hut is the most secure and then the restrictions lessen the farther you get from it." The coven couldn't ward the entire village the same way. They needed magic to survive, even if it was only using the licensed magic in service of the House.

"So, if we're able to break out of here and get across the village, we'd be able to use magic?"

"I think so, yes."

"Then all we need to do is overpower them the next time they bring us food. I'll turn invisible and take them by surprise."

I gave her a pointed look. "Please tell me you noticed the team outside every time they open the door."

"I assumed they were casual observers."

I shook my head. "More like a firing squad."

"Then I suppose we need a cleverer plan."

I laughed. "I'm open to suggestions."

In the end it wasn't Saffron who risked her life to save us. Shouts rang out and I rushed to the window for a look.

"What is it?" London asked, joining me.

Witches and wizards ran in a haphazard fashion as their screams pierced the air.

I was so focused on the chaos outside that I didn't hear the door open and close.

I turned to see Talia. Her pale skin looked almost sickly.

"Talia?" London said.

"Here, put this on. We need to go." She rushed forward and handed us each a black cloak.

My heart lurched as I slipped on the warm material. "What's happening?"

"Vampires. They're searching for you."

Alaric had sent a team. Thank the gods. "Why do we need to go? We'll wait for them to secure the area and then..." The troubled expression on the young witch's face gave me pause.

"They're not here to rescue us, are they?" London asked, clearly knowing the answer.

The young witch shook her head. "They've already killed Gertrude and Anthony. They're demanding to know where you're being held."

The coven wouldn't give up that information without a fight. We were too necessary to their plan.

"Who would send assassins for us?" London asked. "If vampires know, doesn't that mean the king knows?"

My chest tightened as I listened to the growing chaos outside.

"Not necessarily. It's possible they realize Alaric would be at odds with any plan to murder me." But I could understand their desire. If the vampires believed the prophecy, too, then naturally they'd want to kill us and eliminate the possibility of restoring the sun. If they discovered Olis's treachery, it was also possible they kept the information to themselves and opted to handle it quietly, knowing that the king would object.

"The king wouldn't support our assassination, would he?" London asked. "Is there any chance...?"

"None," I said with absolute conviction. I didn't believe in much, but I believed in Alaric's devotion to me.

London seemed to accept my answer. She looked at Talia. "Why haven't they sent anyone to defend us?"

"Because they don't want to reveal your location. They sent reinforcements to a different hut to mislead them."

London nodded. "Okay. What's the best way out of the village? Once we're settled, I can try to open a portal."

"We can't go on foot," I said. I knew Lancaster well

enough to know we wouldn't get far before we were captured.

Shouts grew louder.

"Whatever we do, we need to do it now," London said. "If you need me to turn invisible, I can do that."

The young witch poked her head outside and turned back to us. "You can turn invisible if you want, but it might be easier to stick together if we can see you."

London nodded. "Noted."

Talia inhaled sharply. "All right then. Follow me."

She darted from the hut, and we stayed close behind with our hoods drawn to shield our faces. Everyone was so focused on their own survival that they didn't notice three more in the crowd.

A large barn loomed ahead, and I realized that was our destination. "Is there a car inside?" I asked as we hurried closer. Although we hadn't encountered any vampires yet, I heard the screams of those who had.

"No, but it's the best option for now," Talia insisted. "I have a plan."

"Stop them!" a voice shrieked.

Francesca.

I glanced over my shoulder in time to see a vampire grab her by the throat. Her cries for mercy pierced the air.

"You conspire against our kind," the vampire said. "You deserve no mercy, hag."

"No!" I slowed my run, but London grabbed my arm and pulled me forward.

"You can't. We need to go."

I wouldn't have made it in time anyway. The vampire snapped her neck before she could utter another plea. Fangs bared, his eyes met mine.

"Britt, come on!"

Gunfire pelted the vampire. The coven was fighting back. I didn't wait to see what happened next. I took advantage of the distraction and sprinted for the barn.

"Your plan is to hide in here until what, exactly?" London queried, as we reached the barn. I could tell she was feeling less enthusiastic about our rescue.

Talia closed the double doors behind us and pushed a wooden slat across to secure them. Great. That would hold them back for all of ten seconds.

London made a circular movement with her hand and swore softly. "Barn's warded too. Is there a trap door in here or something?" She rubbed her boot along the floor to check. "Any secret tunnels that take us out of the village?"

"Not that I know of." My gaze slid to Talia, and she shook her head.

"So, we've barricaded ourselves in the barn. One prison for another."

Talia flipped on a light switch and illuminated the interior. "You can hide in one of those until the coast is clear. Then I'll help you. There isn't time right now."

I stared at the rows of larger-than-life-sized clay figures. "What are these?"

"Our hiding spot. Now get in." London removed one of the heads. "Give me a boost."

I clasped my hands together and helped London climb into the figure. I replaced the head. "Can you breathe?"

"Through the eyeholes," she whispered.

"Here," Talia called. She'd already used a stepladder to remove the head of another figure. "Hurry!"

"What about you?" I asked. The vampires would kill her if they found her.

"I'm small enough to hide. I don't need a golem."

The figure was enormous. "There's room for both of us. Hide with me."

Talia slid into the figure first. I followed, still gripping the head, and fastened it over top of us. Although the figure's leg was wide enough for both of us, we huddled together anyway.

"What are these for?" I asked. They certainly hadn't been here when I was a child.

"I'm not sure. A special project."

"There must be three dozen of them."

"They're not finished yet."

In the darkness, I smiled at her. "I gathered that when I took the head off."

"I'd like to come with you when you leave," Talia whispered.

"I appreciate your sunny optimism that we *will* leave, but it would be too dangerous to take you with us."

"You spoke of a place where children live together in harmony."

"Did I say harmony? I'm sure there's infighting..."

"I'm helping you escape and in return I want you to take me there."

I balked. "You want to live in Washington D.C.? Most of those kids are human. You'll be different."

"So what? I'm different here. Maybe I stand a chance of fitting in there. The coven..." Her eyes turned downcast.

I lowered myself to one knee. "What's your skill?"

"I read auras."

I squeezed her hand. "The coven will treat you well. Aura reading is a coveted skill."

"I know that." With her eyes still burning a hole in the ground, she began to chew her lip.

I tipped up her chin so that she met my gaze. "You have another form of magic."

Slowly, she nodded. "They don't know," she whispered. "Reading auras has allowed me to hide it."

"What is it? Whatever it is, I promise I won't judge you for it."

Her swallow of courage was audible. "I can steal magic, but only temporarily. It happens so fast that no one has ever noticed. They blame themselves and try again."

"How do you steal it?" And what did that even mean?

"It isn't as powerful as yours," she explained. "I have to touch the person to activate it."

"And you then possess their magic for a brief timeframe?"

She shook her head. "I only disarm them, but like I said, it's quick. A couple minutes at most."

"Probably because you haven't developed it. I bet if you did, you'd find you can make your magic last longer." What an incredible skill. She was right, though. It was a type of magic the coven would fear. They'd worry about her ability to disarm them all. To take their magic forever.

"They'd see you as a threat," London's voice cut through the moment of contemplative silence.

"You can hear us?" I asked.

"I'm in the golem next door. What do you expect?"

Talia's eyes rounded. Her fear was palpable. "There's something else you should know."

"Go on," I urged. "You can tell us."

"I'm not sure you want to hear this."

I gave her hand a reassuring squeeze. "We're grownups. Whatever it is, we'll deal."

"I can't read your aura. Neither one of you."

"Maybe fear is blocking you," I said. "Strong emotions can sometimes interfere with magic."

She shook her head, adamant. "It isn't me. It's you."

I cast a sidelong glance at the golem wall. "Any theories, London?"

"It could be our unusual magic—or our dismal futures," she added.

"Or the fact that we have no future at all," I said quietly.

"An aura tells me more than your future, though," Talia objected. "It reveals everything about you."

"Everything?" I queried.

A shy smile touched her lips. "Well, it's not like reading your unfiltered autobiography."

I burst into laughter. "Trust me. Nobody wants to read that."

"It's more like emotional information," the young witch continued. "Your body is a container for everything you've experienced up until now and everything you will experience."

"Past, present, and future," I murmured. "What does it look like you to you?"

"Picture yourself in a dark room."

"Not a stretch," I said in a wry tone.

"In the room is a jar with a fairy light trapped inside. The strength and color of the light determine how much of it you can see."

"You can see someone's essence," London said. "Their life-force."

She nodded. "It isn't set in stone, though. An aura can be influenced by the environment or even the auras of others, which is what I thought might have happened to you."

I didn't quite understand. "You thought you couldn't

read us because our auras had been influenced by the coven?"

"Sort of, but also by each other. I thought you might be smudged."

"Smudged?" I wasn't familiar with that term except in connection with burning sage.

"Blocked because of your shared trauma here."

"But you decided we're not...smudged?"

She shook her head. "I've seen blockages before, and this is different. Others I've seen still have auras, but they lack brightness and clarity. Yours are..." She seemed to search for the right word. "Like you exist in a black hole."

I snorted. "Sounds about right."

"Why didn't you tell the coven?" London asked.

"Because I didn't want them to hurt you."

My laughter rang bitter and hollow. "You do realize they're planning to cut out our hearts and light us on fire?"

She dropped her gaze. "I also didn't want them to question my ability. If they decided I was faking my aura reading, they might want to test me for other magic."

Her lie was a matter of self-preservation. That I understood—and respected.

"You have good instincts, little one," I said. "That bodes well for you."

London shushed us. "I hear footsteps."

We fell silent. My heartbeat seemed so loud, I was sure it would reveal our position.

"Here," Talia said quietly. "I took this for you. I'm sorry, I should've given it to you sooner." Her cheeks grew flushed. "It's an important part of the escape plan."

I anticipated the appearance of a small loaf of bread or a bottle of water. "Not to worry, Talia. It's your first time aiding and abetting prisoners." I offered a reassuring smile.

She dipped a hand in her pocket and revealed a familiar red stone attached to a gold chain.

"My necklace," I gasped.

"This is no ordinary necklace," Talia said.

"I know. It was a gift from a goddess."

Talia held up the chain for inspection. "Do you know what it can do?"

"She said it would keep me safe when I traveled through the portal to get home from her realm." I'd acquired it during my Central Park adventure with London.

The young witch offered a triumphant smile. "It can do much more than that."

"How do you know?"

"I overheard one of our librarians talking about it. She considers it a weapon."

I took the shining stone. "How?"

"The amulet has ancient magical properties that can help you leave here."

"But magic won't work. That's the whole point of the ward," I pointed out.

The young witch smiled with satisfaction. "It will when it was crafted by a goddess."

I stared at the red stone as the realization swept over me. "The ancient magic of a goddess trumps that of a coven."

Of course. That difference was what allowed the keelut and heart-eater to break through the ward in New York City. Anat's ancient power overrode the modern magic of witches and wizards.

Sounds of a scuffle drew our attention to the barn doors, followed by more gunfire. Something thumped against the barn. A body?

"What's your plan? To hide here until it seems safe to test the amulet?"

"Once all the vampires have been killed and..."

Oh, to be young and naive again. "Let me stop you right there. There's no luxury of time. If we're going to make a move, we need to make it right now." I should've taken charge when we fled the hut.

The young witch offered a solemn nod. "I'm sorry. I've never planned an escape before."

"Live and learn, kid. Next time, don't bury the lead."

I gave Talia a boost first and then climbed out of the clay figure. London joined us on the floor of the barn.

"If this amulet overrides the ward, I can use magic to get us out of here."

I slipped the chain around London's neck. "Consider it a loan."

Raised voices outside the barn spiked my concern. I turned to London. "How fast can you portal us to D.C.?"

"An unfamiliar destination will take time."

"Then get us somewhere familiar, as long as it's far from here." I noticed Talia examining me closely. "You're reading my aura, aren't you?"

"Still nothing." She clasped my hand. "You can stop worrying, though. You'll get home—eventually."

But where was home for someone like me?

Flecks of gold sparked in the air.

"Where are we going?" I asked.

London moved her hands in a circular fashion. "Somewhere safe until I figure out how to open a portal to D.C."

The barn doors burst open, sending wooden splinters in all directions. Kathleen was the first to barrel through. Her face was twisted with rage and frustration. Blood gushed from a wound on her head. "Stop them!" She sounded hoarse.

"They've got Talia," another voice cried.

Saffron. My sister.

London ushered the young witch through the darkened spiral.

"You bring her back!" Kathleen screamed.

"Not a chance," London said, and quickly followed.

Saffron raised an object in her hand. It took a moment to realize that she'd aimed a shotgun at me. So much for coming around to my side.

"You don't want to do that, Saffron." If only they hadn't warded their own barn, they might have been able to stop me with magic.

"Of course I do. You're an abomination." She squinted, preparing to take the shot. The fact that there wasn't a speck of hesitation was a punch in the gut.

The arrival of vampires interrupted her. Six night-crawlers bulldozed over our attackers, knocking the gun so that Saffron shot a clay figure instead. Kathleen face-planted. I heard the crunch of bone as one of the vampires stepped on her neck on his way toward me. I tried to pinpoint Saffron in the melee but lost sight of her as a vampire approached me with a look of triumph.

There was no more time for gawking. I blew him a farewell kiss and jumped through the portal.

Chapter Three

"What is this place?" It was so bright that I was forced to squint until my eyes were practically closed.

"A pocket dimension of my own creation," London said.

My mouth dropped open. "You created this place? How is that even possible?"

"It's the most beautiful place in the world," Talia cried.

I forced my eyes open for a better view. "Gods above, you've simulated sunlight." Not to mention the meadows that surrounded us.

She bowed. "One of my gifts. If only I could make a real sun."

"Apparently you can," I said with a wry smile. "You just have to die first." I gaped at a passing butterfly. "I take it that's not a vampire."

"Not in this realm."

This realm. "I don't understand."

"It's an alternate plane of existence."

Talia chased the butterfly, laughing. "I never want to leave!"

"It's only a stopover," London told her.

"You can't stay here forever or you'll die," I added.

"That isn't strictly true," London said in a low voice. "I know someone..."

I held up a hand. "Don't tell me. I don't want to put ideas in her head."

"I can get us to D.C. from here, but it'll be faster if you help."

"How can *I* help?"

"You've been there, right? You have a connection to the place?"

"I guess."

"Then that's more than I have." She removed the amulet from around her neck and passed it over my head. "Before I forget."

"Thanks." I touched the red stone and silently thanked the goddess who'd gifted it to me.

"I wish the coven hadn't taken our phones," London said. "We could use them in D.C."

"Olis had likely bugged them when we were unconscious anyway," I said. He'd probably bugged mine even before that.

"Can you call Alaric from D.C. and let him know we're safe?" London asked.

"I can try, but even if I get through, Olis will be ready to intercept my call. Not to mention he'll have all the phones tapped."

"Then call someone who can get a message directly to the king without the risk of interception."

The coven would've warned Olis of our escape by now, assuming the assassins had left any survivors. Olis would expect me to show up in the compound to see Alaric. Liam was the next obvious choice, but Olis knew that, too.

"There is someone I can call."

"Good. I'll call Callan directly. I'm not aware of any infiltration by Trinity Group in our corner of the world."

We were in agreement there. "Seems to be isolated to House August territory."

London scoured the ground.

"What are you looking for?"

"Stones to help with the portal."

"You didn't need stones in the barn."

"Because we were coming here. I've done this so many times now, I can open the door to this realm in record time. It isn't the same for somewhere I haven't been. Takes a bit more out of me."

I trailed after London, collecting stones.

"I've been thinking about what your sister said."

It took me a moment to register the word 'sister.' I didn't know whether she survived. There was every chance she hadn't. "What did she say?"

"About sacrificing herself for the greater good." London paused. "Do you think we're wrong to not consider it?"

I looked at her. "Consider what?"

"What if the coven was right? What if our sacrifice is for the greater good and we should let it happen for her sake?" London motioned to Talia, currently frolicking through the meadow. I knew the word, but I'd never witnessed anyone actually frolic before. It was...uplifting.

"You want to die?" I asked quietly.

"Of course not, but if my death meant something...If I died so that countless others could live." She shrugged. "Isn't that the honor of serving as a knight?"

"I'm not a knight."

"But you have honor. I've seen it."

The laughter that escaped my lips was hollow even to

my own ears. "London, I've done terrible things in the name of survival. There was nothing honorable about my actions."

"I'm not talking about the past. I'm talking about the present. You protected your city when you had no obligation to do so. You protected that little girl when you could've left her behind." She placed a hand on my shoulder. "Like it or not, Britt the Bloody, honor flows through your veins."

"And you think honor means we should let them tie us to a stake, drain our blood, and burn us to death?"

She offered a wry smile. "I admit, it doesn't sound tempting when you put it that way."

I felt conflicted. On the one hand, I understood her point. If we could change the fate of the world for the better, didn't we owe that to the rest of civilization? On the other hand, I wasn't convinced the prophecy was accurate or that Trinity Group was the right organization to call the shots. Leaving the new world order in their hands struck me as risky. I thought of the coven's negative attitude toward those who are different. Their extreme reaction to blood magic.

"I think we'd simply swap one oppressive regime for another. And you and I both know vampires are capable of treating us as more than blood bags."

"Then we have to build a new world order that involves more voices." She dusted off her hands. "Easy peasy."

"Honestly, I think Alaric would be open to it. He doesn't stand on ceremony."

"Sounds like my kind of guy." London arranged the collection of stones. "What's the plan for D.C.? Tell everyone we're safe, drop off Talia, and head our separate ways?"

"I've been mulling it over and I think we'll be setting ourselves up to be targets again."

She flinched. "You think they'll keep coming?"

"Vampire assassins. Trinity Group minions. Face it, London, we're the most wanted witches in the world right now."

"Technically I'm a dhampir."

"As far as they're concerned, you're a point on their prophecy triangle. They won't stop. The stakes are too high."

"Then what do you suggest we do?" she asked, stopping to admire her handiwork.

"I think we should find that dagger Francesca mentioned. It sounds like it's important. No dagger. No ritual."

London stared at me. "But they have teams looking for it."

"So we'll be a team. And if we encounter them in the wild, we'll have our magic." I smiled. "I think we've already established we make a pretty good team."

She nodded. "That we do." She gestured to the rock circle. "Ready when you are."

I called Talia and the young witch reluctantly joined us. "Can't this be D.C.?"

"Unfortunately not," I said. "Not enough of a wasteland."

"Give it time," London said.

Talia's hands pressed against her small hips. "Well, aren't you two a bucket full of cheer?"

London crooked a finger. "Come on, little miss. Time to go."

Talia joined her in the circle. "Is this really what sunlight would be like?"

"I think so," London said. "Hard to say for certain though. It's only my best guess based on descriptions I've read."

Talia sat cross-legged and faced her. "Did you know Japan was once called Land of the Rising Sun? They must've really struggled with a new nickname during the Eternal Night."

"I did know that, in fact," London said. "And Norway was Land of the Midnight Sun, so they had to find themselves a new moniker too."

I added myself to the circle and watched in awe as she worked her magic. They were wrong about London. She wasn't an abomination.

She was a miracle.

The District of Columbia looked better than I'd left it. There'd been obvious progress with buildings and there was no sign of monsters, which was the biggest change to the region. Once an abandoned wasteland, D.C. was beginning to enjoy a resurgence thanks to the influx of orphans determined to create a home for themselves.

"Are we going to the actual White House?" Talia asked as the white structure came into view.

"That's where Twila is, so yes."

"Who's Twila?"

"A friend." Alaric and I had discovered her in an underground lair, imprisoned by her wizard boss. After we freed her, Twila decided to stay and look after the children. She was the Wendy to their Lost Boys—and girls.

The White House was almost fully intact. The paint didn't all match—different shades of white based on age—but the building was once again structurally sound.

Children were running riot when we entered. There didn't seem to be any form of security, not that I was surprised. It would take time for the city's reputation as a wasteland to change. For all most people knew, the Monster Maze was still active.

"Hi," a boy greeted us. "Can I help you?" He looked at Talia. "Have you come to stay with us?"

Talia glanced at me for approval. "This is Talia," I said. "She's planning to stay. Could you point me in the direction of Twila?"

He gestured toward the west wing. "She's working on the menu for next week. We have to plan ahead or we don't eat." He said this somewhat cheerily, as though he'd heard it so often that it couldn't possibly be true.

"Will you be all right here?" I asked.

"Come on," the boy said. "I'll show you the maze. There used to be monsters there but not anymore."

Talia smiled. "Thank you."

I touched my necklace. "No, thank you for being brave."

She ran off and London and I continued along the corridor until we located Twila.

"Is this an illusion?" she asked, gaping at me. She sat behind a desk with dozens of papers scattered across it.

"Surprise," I said. "This is my friend, London."

London wiggled her fingers in greeting.

"We need your help."

Twila skirted the desk. She bounded forward and threw her arms around me. "Anything for you. You're my hero."

"London and I are in danger. I need to get a message to Alaric without going through the proper channels."

"I don't understand. Why not call the compound?"

I sighed. "I can't. His Director of Security will likely have all the royal phone lines tapped, listening for my voice or my name. He'll find a way to shut down the call or trace it."

"Then who do you want to call?"

"That's where you come in. I'd like you to call Roger." Roger Akers was the king's best friend. Even better, he lived in Palm Beach, not the city compound.

"If I can call Roger, why not let me call the king?" Twila asked.

"Because a young woman calling Roger in the Southern Territories will suffer far less scrutiny. And you won't mention my name."

"Won't Roger's call to Alaric be monitored, too?" London asked.

"Roger and Alaric have a long-standing friendship and a way of communicating that bypasses royal protocol." Alaric's womanizing days might actually work in my favor.

I explained what to say and had her use the speakerphone setting so I could listen.

"I need to speak with Roger," Twila said in a more high-pitched voice.

"I'm afraid Mr. Akers is only accepting important calls at the moment," an unfamiliar voice said.

"My mother told me the king is my father, so I'd classify that as fairly important, wouldn't you?" Twila winked at me.

I gave her a thumbs up.

"One moment, please."

I tapped my foot impatiently. *Come on, Roger. Answer the phone.*

"This is Roger."

My stomach unclenched.

"Hi, Roger. I understand you're the man to speak to about the king's indiscretions," Twila said.

"I see. Do me a favor and call me at this number. It offers more...discretion."

Perfect.

She hung up and scribbled down the number.

I immediately dialed it.

"This is Roger."

I practically jumped out of my skin in my eagerness to speak to him. "Roger, it's me. Don't say my name." Even if the line was secure, I couldn't risk him being overheard.

"All right then. How's travels? Find a good spot to put down roots yet or have you come to your senses?"

He didn't know what happened, which meant Alaric didn't either.

"Listen, Roger. Are you alone? If not, I need you go somewhere you can talk with absolute privacy."

"Got it. Give me one minute."

My heart pounded as I waited. One minute seemed to stretch into an eternity.

"I'm as secure as I'm going to be."

"Where are you?" I could hear the roar of the ocean in the background.

"On the beach. There was a kraken sighting earlier so nobody wants to be near the water. I'll risk it for you."

Gods, I adored Roger. "Listen carefully. I haven't been traveling. I was taken against my will by Olis and his people. Trinity Group is behind it. I'm with another witch taken at the same time."

"This is why you had to get me on a secure line. Who's the witch?"

"I don't want to say names."

"Can you rhyme it?"

"Not easily. It was the former name of Britannia City."

"Where you are now?"

I hesitated. "I don't want to say more than I have to."

"Understood. Tell me what I can do. I can't believe Olis would betray the House."

"He's been biding his time. Building their trust until the time came when he could exploit it."

"I'll try to reach Alaric on our secure line, but I have to be honest, since you came back into his life, it hasn't been in use. He may not answer."

"It's worth a try. It's the only direct line to him that won't be monitored." I paused. "When you speak to him, ask if he's seen George or Liam."

"George isn't with you?"

"No, and I'm worried Olis did something to him and Liam."

"Anything else you want me to tell him?"

"That I can't come back to New York yet, but I will as soon as I can." I didn't want to mention the dagger and give Trinity Group a heads up. "Call him now and then call me right back, okay? I need to know that he got the message."

"Okay."

I hung up and waited. A few minutes later the phone rang.

"No answer," Roger said. "I didn't want to leave a voicemail, so I'll call again."

My spirits deflated. "We can't leave this too long."

"I know, that's why I'm going to keep calling from the train."

"The train?"

"I'll call every hour until I reach New York, and if I don't get him on the phone, I'll deliver the information in person."

I almost burst into tears. "You're the best, Roger Akers. Alaric doesn't know how lucky he is."

"Trust me, he knows."

"Don't go to the compound. Have him meet you somewhere else. Olis won't suspect the two of you going out for a night on the town during your visit."

"I'll let you know where and when in case you can make an appearance."

The thought of seeing Alaric again was too much to bear. "Stay safe," I whispered and disconnected.

London looked at me. "He seems nice."

"The nicest."

London used the phone to call Callan and explain what happened. Based on the distance she held the phone from her ear, the king was unhappy with the news.

"Let King Alaric handle his own House business," London insisted. "You can't ring him or you'll put Britt at risk." She paused to listen. "I haven't decided yet. We need to figure out a few things first. I miss you, too." She returned the phone to me. "He was most displeased."

"I could tell."

Now I needed to call someone else whose number I didn't have memorized. I tried to conjure the images of the numbers, but they refused to come.

I heaved a sigh. "I can't get in touch with Meghan." Meghan was a werewolf whose husband I'd killed during my time as an assassin. His vampire family hadn't approved of their match and had decided to eliminate that branch of the family before it could bear fruit. Meghan had searched for me for years, swearing vengeance. Thankfully, our time together turned out much different than either of us expected.

Twila perked up. "Meghan? Why didn't you say so? I have her number. She's been here to visit the children a few times."

This was news to me. "She has?"

Twila nodded. "She helped build the stable for the horses, which was pretty funny considering how well she and horses get along."

"Her number's programmed in here? 'M' for Meghan?"

Twila smiled. "'W' for werewolf."

"Doesn't that get tricky with 'W' for witches and wizards?"

"Not really. I don't call any of them."

Sure enough, I found Meghan under 'W' and hit the call button. I'd last told her I'd leave our communication in her hands, but this was an urgent matter. London and I could use a tracker, but I couldn't risk contacting Liam, even if I could.

The number was out of order.

"Are you sure this is the right number?" I asked.

Twila frowned. "Definitely, although I guess she might've switched numbers without telling me."

That was too bad. Now I might never get the chance to make amends. Of course, asking her for a favor probably wasn't the best way to achieve that anyway.

"What next?" Twila asked. "Tell me how I can help."

My stomach rumbled. "Do you have any food?"

Only after I ate could I think clearly. London didn't seem to need as much food as I did. Maybe her vampire side afforded her a different metabolism.

We remained sequestered in Twila's office, eating whatever was set in front of us. I told Twila about Talia and arranged for her to be fed and housed as well. I let her know the young witch could read auras, but I left the rest for Talia to share if and when she felt ready. Her secret wasn't mine to reveal.

"Is there a library nearby?" London asked. "Somewhere we could research the location of the dagger?"

Twila perked up. "The Library of Congress was once the world's largest library."

"And it's here?" London asked, her face registering shock.

"Well, remnants of it," Twila said, "which is still pretty good if it was once the largest."

"Worth a shot," I said. "We just need a couple leads to get us started."

Twila bit her lip. "There's one small problem."

"What is it?"

"There's a teeny tiny monster issue there."

"What are you talking about? All the monsters are gone from the wasteland."

She wore a sheepish expression. "Except this one group, but they don't tend to leave the library, so it hasn't been an issue."

"Why haven't they left?" London asked.

"They feed on the microbes found on paper. I figure the library will keep them busy until we decipher a way to kill them off."

"Which species?" London asked.

"Tamandua cyclops."

London frowned. "Never heard of them."

"You don't have them on your continent. They came up from South America. Knuckle walkers. They've got faces like anteaters which I think is how they got their name. Oh, and one eye, of course."

"So they hoover up the microbes with their elongated snouts?" London asked.

"Pretty much."

"What's the danger level?" I asked.

Twila ticked off the items on her fingers. "Claws. Climbers. Excellent scenting ability."

"Doesn't sound too bad," I mused.

"Oh, and they're about the size of elephants."

I blinked. "How did we miss them the first time around?"

"They lay low unless their territory is threatened, which we discovered when we tried to scout out some new reading material for the kids. Let's just say they would not loan us any books."

"Large and in charge. Got it. What do you have for weapons?"

London cracked her knuckles. "Don't need any weapons this time. Leave them to me."

I looked at Twila. "You mentioned a group. How many of them would you say are there?"

"Not sure. We saw three, but I got the sense there were more."

"Do you think there's a way you might co-exist?" London asked. "If they eat microbes, maybe they're not a threat to you?"

"I'm mainly worried about what they'll eat once they're through all the books. Will they try to suck the microbes off our bodies and kill us in the process?" Twila shrugged. "I'll be honest, don't want to find out the hard way."

"Fair enough." She slapped her hands on the desk. "Ready when you are, Britt."

The Library of Congress was once comprised of three buildings. London and I headed to the Thomas Jefferson Building, which was the most intact of the trio and therefore the most likely to have well-preserved books.

"You could just turn invisible and carry out a few books that look promising," I told London outside the building.

"They'll smell me. They have good noses, remember?"

"True." I contemplated the partially collapsed building. "How do monsters the size of elephants live in such a small area? I mean, the buildings are big to us, but..." My musings were interrupted by the sound of stomping. A Tamandua cyclops rounded the corner and ambled toward us. Based on its size, I guessed it was more of a toddler. It didn't seem threatening, but I knew well that looks could be deceiving.

The creature was very much as described. A knuckle-dragging elephant with a narrower anteater's head. No big, flappy ears like Dumbo.

London glanced at me. "I'm thinking we let him inspect us if he wants to."

I nodded.

The toddler approached London first, using his elongated snout to sniff what seemed like every inch of her. He seemed curious, which only made me think of George. I felt a pang of longing for the phoenix and prayed he was unharmed.

I was next. The single eye was unsettling at first, but I quickly grew accustomed to it. The snout dragged along my arm and then investigated my hair. I laughed at the tickling sensation along my scalp.

"Hey, we're getting a deep clean out of this," London said softly. "I call it a win no matter what."

"Are you sure we need to do anything with these creatures?" I asked. "They seem fine."

"This guy's fine. He's not the one you need to worry about, though."

The creature continued inside the building, and London and I followed behind him. It was a good thing London and I were adept at research because the number of books in the library was staggering, not to mention the disarray caused by the resident monsters and whatever else ran through here after the Great Eruption. The place reeked of excrement and I had to stifle my gag reflex more than once.

"I thought the rule was not to shit where you eat," I complained.

"Monsters follow different rules."

"Monsters don't follow any rules. That's part of what makes them monsters."

She smirked. "Shows how much you know about them."

Our first attempt at research was interrupted by the arrival of two more Tamandua cyclops.

"Two females," London said. "My guess is mother and daughter." She stopped moving. "Stay still and let them inspect you, same as before."

These two weren't as playful as the toddler. The older female in particular seemed aggravated. She grunted her disapproval more than once as she examined me. When her claw threatened to slice my arm open, I darted out of reach.

"Now might be a good time to 'win them over,' as you say," I told London.

The older female made a sound at the base of her throat.

"Distress signal," London said. "Not good. Give me a minute." She focused on the mother first. Although I couldn't *see* any magic, I could tell something was happening. The older female stopped making noise and settled down, finally ambling over to lay her snout on London's shoulder. London rubbed the snout as she continued to make connections with the other two creatures.

"They're sweethearts," she said, once she'd finished. "I definitely think they can work with the children here rather than against them. Form a symbiotic relationship."

"I'm sure Twila will be happy to hear that." It couldn't be easy keeping so many children clean and free of microorganisms. The Tamandua cyclops could help with that important task.

Once the creatures had fully warmed to us, we decided to divide and conquer. There were more books than I could count, and it wasn't easy to find the relevant ones since they were no longer in their proper order. If I saw a nonfiction book that might mention a Blade of Fire, I went straight to the index for a quick look. The toddler seemed interested in my research and kept me company for the next couple hours.

The floor rumbled and I thought it might be an earthquake until I heard London say, "Uh oh. Looks like daddy's home."

The missing male member of the group charged into the library. London turned to focus her energy on the angry monster. He was twice the size of the mother, his claws included. The air rushed past me as the other family members hurried to form a wall between us and the returning male. The female made soft grunting noises in an effort to calm her mate.

London and I remained perfectly still with our backs to the wall and waited for the crisis to pass.

"Are you going to work your mojo on him?" I whispered.

"I'd rather wait and see if they won't do it for us. His partner's making a pretty good case for us, it seems."

She was. The male relaxed and dragged his knuckles toward us with far less aggression than when he'd entered the building.

"Do we let him inspect?" I asked, careful not to turn my head too quickly.

"Yes, same as before," London said.

The male probed a bit more with his snout, go figure. He remained a gentleman, however.

When it was her turn, London took time staring into the creature's eye.

"Are you forming a connection after all?" I asked.

"A natural one. Not a magical one." She smoothed the creature's short hair. "I think the children would be all right coming here now. The library would be a wonderful place for them to explore."

"You don't think the creatures will feel threatened?"

"We've reached an understanding." She smiled at the male. "Haven't we, friend?"

The creature lowered his head and she gave him a playful swat. "Go on then. Let us get back to work. We've got a dagger in a haystack to find."

No kidding. I waded into a pile of books on the floor and began to pick through them. The pages were clean, I'd say that much for them.

I flipped to the index of yet another tome which promised to answer our questions about the dagger. My stomach lurched.

"Here it is! Blade of Fire." The listing also identified the obsidian dagger by multiple other names in languages I didn't recognize.

London came to read over my shoulder. "Anything useful?"

I nearly threw the book across the room when I arrived at the relevant page to find only a passing mention of it in relation to mythological weapons.

"Wait," London urged as I raised my arm to hurl the book. "Go back. I saw another mention of it further down the page."

I lowered the book and followed her finger to the relevant paragraph. It wasn't much, but at least it was more than a passing reference.

"Although the location of the dagger remains a mystery, it's widely believed to be hidden in the Yellowstone Caldera where it's protected by mystical forces. It was said that whoever wielded the dagger would hold the world in the palm of their hand."

"I have no idea what that means," London said.

"Me neither. Doesn't sound accurate." But it was all the information we had. "Yellowstone Caldera is technically in House Nilsson territory." Although it wasn't a high occupancy area thanks to the destruction that followed the Great Eruption.

"Is House Nilsson good or bad?" London asked.

"Is anybody all good or bad? I can't vouch for the king and queen, but there's a pair of royal twins I can count on if we run into trouble there." Genevieve and Michael had been instrumental in our battle against the Pey.

"Should we start there then?"

I closed the book. "Every journey begins with a single step. What do you think? Can you portal us to Yellowstone?"

London shrugged. "Only one way to find out."

Chapter Four

We discovered the hard way that London could not, in fact, portal us directly to Yellowstone Caldera.

"Nobody's perfect," I said in an effort to ease any guilt she might be feeling. "What is this place?"

We stood at the edge of a body of water.

"Ocean?" she ventured.

I scooped water into my hand and tasted it. "Interesting. Not quite freshwater but not too high in salinity either. One of the Great Lakes?"

London scanned the horizon. "Not a Great Lake. Those are freshwater. Anyway, see those mountains in the distance?"

I peered across the water. "Vaguely."

"Those are the Rocky Mountains, which makes this the Western Interior Seaway. We need to cross it to get to Yellowstone." She gazed at the water. "This divide was here during the Cretaceous period, but it disappeared over time, only to reemerge during the Great Eruption. It's not the exact same waterway, of course, but similar."

"Wow. You're full of fun facts."

"That's what happens when you have a mother who was a history teacher."

I felt mildly embarrassed that London knew more about my continent than I did. Then again, she had an expert for a mother, and I had...one that elected to discard me when I ceased to fit the mold of a witch.

"Now for the fun part," London continued. "How are we going to cross this? See anything we can use?"

"We can't portal?"

London snorted. "I think we're better off taking our chances on the back of a sea monster at this point. The destination is too amorphous."

I searched the area for anything we could use as a flotation device. "I see nothing useful."

"Except a giant ship?" London suggested.

"Hardy har. If only."

"No, seriously. There's a giant ship headed our way."

I turned to follow her gaze and saw the ship sailing toward us. A black flag blew in the breeze, and it was only when the fabric stopped rippling for a moment that I noticed the skull and crossbones.

"There be pirates," London said.

"I noticed. "

"Should we hide?"

"You can turn invisible. The best I can do is stand very still."

"Maybe they're the entrepreneurial type who'll give us a lift," London said.

"In exchange for what? We don't have any money." And I didn't think it was wise to offer pirates any favors in return. That kind of offer could easily be misconstrued.

"How on earth did they spot us in the pitch dark?" I asked as I watched a dinghy drop from the side of the ship.

"Because they keep a lookout. You can't loot what you can't see." She cut me a glance. "Don't worry. I think between the two of us we can take a bunch of pirates if necessary. Even with weapons, they're only human."

"You want to chance it then?"

"You want to get across, don't you? This ship is our best bet."

I nodded. She was right; we could handle ourselves.

We waited as a single figure rowed to shore. He didn't seem to be in much of a hurry, so I guess he wasn't worried that we'd turn tail and run.

"He's whistling," London said under her breath.

I could just make out the tune of Yankee Doodle Dandy.

Once the dinghy was close enough to shore, London and I waded through the shallow water to speak to him. He wore a bright yellow bandana. Instead of a pierced ear, he had a small gemstone shining on each fang.

"Vampire pirates. Even better," I mumbled.

"Ahoy there," he said. "Get in. Captain's orders."

London rolled her eyes. "Sure, we'll play." She climbed into the boat first and I followed suit. The pirate slid to the middle, forcing me apart from London.

"I always dreamed of a threesome," he said with a lascivious grin.

"Well, enjoy it while you can because this is close as you're going to get," I said.

He laughed as he rowed us to the ship. "My name's Daryl."

"Sounds about right," I said.

"What are two ladies like yourselves doing in such a dangerous place?"

"This place doesn't seem very dangerous," London said. She dragged a hand through the water. "Just wet."

"Oh, I wouldn't recommend that if I was you. All sorts of monsters in the murk. They'll smell you a mile away." He began to row faster, which suggested he wasn't simply trying to scare us.

We pulled alongside the ship without incident and climbed the rope ladder, where we were welcomed aboard by the captain himself. The vampire was taller than the others and in lieu of the headscarves, tattoos, and piercings of his crew members, this black-haired vampire wore a white suit lined with rhinestones and a pair of snakeskin boots. The only thing that identified him as the captain of this illustrious ship was the name tag that simply read 'Captain.'

"Who've we got with us, Daryl?" the captain asked.

"Dunno. Didn't ask their names. Just told them mine."

The captain grunted his disapproval. "Daryl, go swab the deck."

"But I swabbed yesterday," Daryl complained.

The captain gave him a sharp look that motivated Daryl to grab a mop on his way to the deck.

"Nice outfit," I remarked. "Very retro."

He adjusted his cuffs. "They say dress for the job you want, right?"

"And you want to be an Elvis impersonator?" I asked.

"Who said anything about impersonations? Captain Presley at your service. Thank you very much."

I stifled a laugh, prompting a sharp look from the captain.

"Is my name funny to you?"

"Do you want an honest answer to that?"

He regarded me with narrowed eyes. "No."

"Didn't think so."

"Why are you lovely ladies hoping to cross my waterway?" he demanded.

I widened my eyes in mock surprise. "Oh, is this your waterway? I thought it belonged to House Nilsson."

The captain blew a raspberry. "Poppycock. The waterway is ours, but we'll let you cross it...for a price." He dragged a craggy fingernail down his cheek. "But first I'd like to know your destination."

"We're looking for something," I said.

"Aren't we all? Story of my life, babe."

"Nothing philosophical or metaphysical. An actual something."

"Do tell. If it's treasure you're after, we may be able to assist you."

"Not treasure." I didn't want to tell him it was a weapon, though. That might pique his interest as much as treasure.

"We're headed to Yellowstone Caldera," London interjected.

Captain Presley scratched his chin. "I haven't heard of any treasure buried there. Have you, Erik?" He turned to the strapping vampire behind him. Erik's long, blond hair was tied with a black bow at the base of his neck. With his broad shoulders and muscular biceps, he seemed born to plunder and pillage.

"No, Captain," Erik said. "No treasure in Yellowstone to my knowledge." His voice was smooth like whiskey.

"This is my mate, Erik," the captain said.

"Your first mate?"

"No, my mate as in life partner." He turned and kissed the Viking pirate.

"Congratulations," London said. "You did well for yourself."

"We know what it's like to be attracted to authority figures," I said.

"Oh, I wasn't drawn to him because of his position as captain," Erik said. "It was the way he sings. His voice is like a choir of angels."

"Well, you can't drop that bombshell and not sing for us," I told them.

The captain wrinkled his nose. "Really? You want to hear me sing?"

London and I were effusive in our entreaties.

Captain Presley seemed to enjoy the attention. Color me shocked that a vampire pirate in a white rhinestone suit would enjoy being fawned over. "If you insist. Why don't you join me in my stateroom, and we can further discuss your request for transport?"

"The ship's already moving toward the other side," London pointed out.

"Maybe so, but I can order us to turn off course at any time." He smiled. "The beauty of being this guy." He tapped the name tag affixed to his suit.

We trailed behind him to the stateroom where he plucked a black guitar from its position on the wall.

He looked at us expectantly. "Any requests?"

"My Way?" I suggested. It was a song that reminded me of New York and Alaric. It would be a comfort to hear it right now.

"Excellent choice." The captain seemed surprised by the suggestion. He performed it admirably, but his talent seemed more in his hips than his voice. Lucky Erik.

Once he finished the song and waited for the proffered applause, he set the guitar aside. "Now, tell me more about yourselves so that I can decide whether or not to eat you."

It was hard to take him seriously in that outfit.

London answered first. "I'm London Hayes, a Knight of Boudica. Consort of King Callan."

I was wondering whether she'd mention her connection to the crown. It could work for us or against us with vampire pirates. Hard to tell.

He examined London closely. "A king who's chosen a human?"

"Not a human," she replied.

"Ah, that makes more sense. You don't smell like a wet dog, so you must be a witch."

She didn't correct him, not that I expected her to.

"One of the reasons I enjoy the seaway is because I don't have to answer to any House. Crowns change heads. I simply steer north, south, east or west. Whatever my heart desires." He looked London up and down. "I must say, you're not how I'd expect a knight to look."

"Right back at you, Captain."

"I'm Britt," I said. "I was once a servant for House August, but I no longer serve the crown."

"And are you a witch, too?"

I nodded.

"Two lovely ladies on the open road." He exhaled dramatically. "Sounds like a good time. Please tell me you've run away together."

"We have, but not in the way you think," I said.

"Too bad. I'm a sucker for an against-all-odds love story." He returned the guitar to the wall. "Tell me about this object you seek in Yellowstone."

Before I could answer, my stomach growled.

Captain Presley recoiled in horror. "What sort of host am I? I haven't offered you hospitality."

"If you offer us hospitality, does that mean you can't kill us?" I asked.

"There are no rules on the Western Interior Seaway," he replied. "Well, only the ones I devise." He smiled again and this time I noticed the sharpness of his fangs. I couldn't let his friendly manner fool me. There was a shrewd killer underneath all those rhinestones. He was simply waiting for the right moment to reveal himself. I got the sense he liked to make an entrance.

He called to a crew member and ordered them to feed us. I had no idea what kind of food to expect on a ship of vampire pirates.

"Sit, ladies. I insist. You're my guests." He motioned to the black lacquer table at the side of the stateroom.

"I wouldn't have expected such shiny furniture on a pirate ship," London said as she lowered herself into the matching chair.

"I've been sailing for many years," the captain said. "When I see a piece I like better, I swap them. This stateroom has been redone fifty times over. At one point, I had a lava lamp and a disco ball hanging from the ceiling." He laughed. "I like to keep things interesting aboard the Jailhouse Rock."

I blanched. "I'm sorry. I must've missed that. Did you say the ship is named Jailhouse Rock?"

He winked. "Get it? We're all trapped on here and it rocks from side to side." He demonstrated the movement.

"Oh, I get it." If London and I had to kill these guys, I was going to feel damn sorry about it.

A crew member arrived with a covered tray. He set it on the table and the captain urged him to remove the lid. I was pleased to see two bowls of hearty soup teeming with vegetables, as well as a carafe of red wine and a loaf of crusty bread. Perfect.

"Bon appetite, my friends," the captain said. "Oh wait. Spencer, you forgot the cutlery!"

"Why do you have all this?" London asked. "Are there other species among your crew?"

"No, we always keep food on board for guests and the wine is enjoyed by all of us. Beer doesn't keep as long."

I lifted the bowl to my lips and slurped the soup. I was too hungry to wait for a spoon. It occurred to me that the guests to which the captain referred were akin to Hansel and Gretel being fed by the witch in order to fatten them up.

I set down the bowl and looked at London. "We're Hansel and Gretel."

"You're just getting that now?"

Spencer reappeared with the cutlery, and I ate the remaining soup with the provided spoon.

"Who are Hansel and Gretel?" the captain asked.

"A couple of children we know," I said. I drained the red wine from the glass without pausing for breath. How I'd missed it.

"I never thought I'd drink again after what Olis did," London said, drinking her wine with more restraint than I'd shown.

"You haven't drugged us, have you?" I asked.

The captain shrugged. "If I have, it's too late to do anything about it."

I reached for his blood just to see if I could tap into it. He seemed to sense I was up to something because he jumped to his feet. "Relax, I haven't drugged you. Frankly, the suggestion is insulting." He swilled his wine. "My crew usually enjoys a good story after supper. I don't suppose you'd like to hear one."

"I'd love to hear one," London enthused. "I'll be sure to share the story with my banner when I get home. The knights love a good tale."

The captain summoned Erik, as well as a few of the crew members to join us in the stateroom. It seemed to be an honor to be invited.

"As the storyteller, I hold the talking stick." The captain held up a decorated wooden stick about eight inches long.

"Is it wise to hold a stake that close?" London asked.

He clutched the stick to his chest. "This is not a stake. It's a *talking stick*."

"You won't be doing much talking if somebody stakes you with it," I quipped.

He shot me an annoyed look. "Do you want to hear the story or not? If so, then be quiet." He waved the stick in the air. "I am the only one with the authority to speak right now."

London and I exchanged amused looks.

"Once upon a time, there was a brilliant sun in the sky, and that sun was held up by thousands of hummingbirds."

I squinted at him. "Hummingbirds? Not butterflies?"

He shushed me. "No interruptions!" He shook the stick at me. "The hummingbirds were the souls of fallen warriors."

"It is similar to butterflies," London whispered. "People used to believe that a butterfly symbolized a departed soul."

The captain glared at her but continued his story. "The hummingbirds kept the sun in the perfect position so that no shadows fell upon the earth. Nothing to remind the inhabitants of the terrifying demons of the night."

Erik made a spooky sound as he delivered another carafe of wine to the table.

"Every evening, the sun was devoured by monsters of the earth," the captain said. "People awaited a new day with trepidation because there was always that moment of transition between dark and light that scared them. That possibility, however remote, that the sun would not rise."

"We know all about that," London murmured.

"And so, people decided to safeguard against such outcomes by offering sacrifices to the gods."

I rolled my eyes. "Of course they did. Let me guess. Young girls were their favorite offering."

"You'll be happy to know the descendants of these same people eventually decided the sacrifices were too 'uncivilized.'" He used air quotes around the word. "And now look what happened. No sun. These people ended up sacrificing themselves." The vampire slapped his knee, guffawing. "The cruel irony of it all."

"Do you believe the story?" I asked. "That the sacrifices were the reason the sun continued to rise?"

He pulled a face. "Come on now. Do I look gullible to you? Of course not."

I leaned forward, my head buzzing from the wine. "What if I told you there was a prophecy that involved a sacrifice which would, in fact, bring back the sun?"

"Then I would tell you..." He paused to belch. "Poppycock." His lips popped on the pronunciation of each 'p.'

London regarded him curiously. "You don't believe in magic?"

He swirled his wine, nearly spilling it in the process. "Hard to believe in something you never see."

I took another sip of wine. It tasted mildly acidic, but I wouldn't have expected a pirate ship to have quality wine.

"You can't see the sun, yet you believe one exists, right? Or at least existed at one time?"

"How do you think plants continue to grow?" London interjected. "There's magic all around you. The entirety of vampire society is built on magic. They just don't like to acknowledge it too loudly or the witches and wizards might grow bold."

"And what? Challenge vampire authority?" The captain threw his head back and laughed, prompting the rest of the crew to do the same.

"Why do you think vampires have suppressed our magic for so long?" I asked. "They're terrified of losing power to our kind."

"I don't think so," Erik said. "If any species is poised to take over, it's shifters."

Captain Presley twisted to face him. "Why do you say that, my love?"

"They're already organized. They're strong and fast. They can howl, like really loudly."

"They're not organized enough to stage a coup. The Houses keep the wolves from organizing into packs for that very reason," I pointed out.

"I wouldn't object to a strong werewolf king," Erik mused.

Captain Presley cast a sidelong glance at him. "I thought we talked about your lupine fantasies."

"And you agreed to invest in a fur coat," Erik said, leaning forward to nibble the captain's ear.

The vampire leader pushed the empty carafe across the table to Erik. "More, please, my darling."

"As you wish." Erik rose from the table with the empty pitcher.

"How old are you?" I asked, genuinely curious.

"How old do I look?"

"Centuries."

His smile broadened. "You're too kind." Snickering, he lowered his voice. "As it happens, you're correct."

"Why don't you have any silver or white streaks?" London asked. "Your hair is jet black."

He put a finger to his lips. "I may be covering them."

"Why?" Most vampires wanted the world to know they were old. Age meant longevity and power.

He glanced over his shoulder at Erik, who was focused on refilling the carafe. "Erik finds older vampires intimidating. He thinks we're much closer in age."

"You know, trust is the basis of a healthy relationship," I told him.

Captain Presley waved a dismissive hand. "Good sex is the basis of a healthy relationship."

It was hard to hear the word 'sex' without thinking of Alaric. I pushed down thoughts of the vampire king. If the gods were kind, I'd be reunited with him soon. Right now, I had to focus on the task at hand—not dying at the hands of vampire pirates. No matter how entertaining they were, they were still deadly and unpredictable.

"Leave us," the captain said suddenly. "Except you, Erik. You may stay."

The crew members grumbled their displeasure as they filed out of the stateroom.

"Now that we're alone again," the captain said, "I'd like you to tell me about the treasure you seek."

I cast a sidelong glance at London, and she nodded her approval.

I rested my hands on the table. "Here's the deal. The prophecy I told you about is real. London and I are doomed to be sacrificed, along with a third witch we don't know.

There's a sacrificial dagger out there designated for this purpose. That's what they plan to use to kill us during the ritual."

"What's so special about this dagger?" Erik asked. "Is it made of diamonds?"

"Obsidian from one of the supervolcanoes that blew during the Great Eruption," London said.

"Obsidian," Erik repeated. "I've never heard of it. Is it like opal?"

"Erik, my love, stop talking for a bit," the captain said. He returned his attention to me. "Now I understand why you want to find it."

"We remove a critical piece from the board, then no chance for that particular prophecy to come to fruition."

"What did you say the name of this dagger was?" he asked.

I looked at him. "What makes you think it has a name?"

He chuckled awkwardly. "My dear, a thing like that must always have a name."

"The Blade of Fire," I said.

Recognition flashed in his eyes.

"You know it," I said, not bothering to frame it as a question. I was too excited.

He averted his gaze. "I may have heard mention of it."

Erik gave his partner a playful smack. "You remember, my love. Those wizards we killed. They spoke of it."

London and I exchanged uneasy glances. "When was this?" I dared to ask.

"Maybe ten days ago. Two weeks, tops," Erik rambled, seemingly oblivious to the captain's critical eye. "They didn't say what it was for, only that they were tasked with retrieving it as the collectors of artifacts for their coven."

"What else did they tell you?" I asked, trying my best

not to sound too eager. I didn't trust Captain Presley to share freely.

"Now that kind of information is going to cost you." He cracked a smile.

"I'm open to negotiations," I said. "Name your price."

"That necklace you wear is very pretty," he said.

My hand covered the amulet from the goddess. "Not for sale. What else?"

"Sentimental value?" he pressed.

"Very. I consider it my good luck charm."

Erik clapped the captain on the shoulder. "And he is mine."

"Why did you kill them?" London asked. "The wizards."

"Why else? We were hungry," the captain replied.

"We threw them overboard when we were done," Erik said. "We don't like to keep the scraps aboard. It attracts creatures we prefer to keep at bay."

The captain shifted in annoyance. "They said they thought they would find the dagger buried in the caldera, but they learned during their journey that it's elsewhere. We picked them up on the Wyoming border, in fact."

"Elsewhere?" I prompted.

"One of the calderas in South America," Erik offered. "Isn't that right? They were worried how they'd survive the journey." He broke into fits of laughter. "Oh, the irony."

"Is that what you're doing to us?" I asked. "Lulling us into a false sense of security?"

Captain Presley gave me a long look. "I honestly haven't decided yet."

I opted not to continue that thread of conversation for the time being, not while I had burning questions. "Did they say which caldera in South America?"

"No, but they discussed organizing more teams," the captain said. "It all sounded incredibly tedious."

"They said nobody would be able to walk up and take it," Erik chimed in. "There'd be tests."

London heaved a deep sigh. "There are always tests."

"Any idea what kind?" I asked.

The captain finished his wine. "They were told the challenges are based on the hazards a soul might face in each level of the underworld, but the wizard who told us wasn't sure he believed it."

"Did you happen to ask their names?" I asked. I wondered whether the team had been from Trinity Group or Lancaster.

"Didn't bother," the captain said.

"Why not? You asked us ours," I said.

"Because I had no doubt what would become of them," he said with a rock-hard expression. "To be perfectly frank, I don't fancy a return of the sun."

"Why not kill us then?" London asked. "That would be a guarantee."

He contemplated us. "It's more sporting to let you try and fail."

"You're lying," I said. "Tell us the truth. Why aren't you interested in stopping us?"

He glanced at the door to the stateroom as though not wanting to be overheard. "Because we're outsiders like you and I have a firm policy of not punching down."

"What makes you think we're outsiders?" London asked.

The captain snorted. "Don't insult my intelligence, lovely lady. If your heads are destined to be on spikes, you're not the belles of the ball now, are you? There must be something different about you. Something that gives those wizards an incentive to kill their own kind and be able to look at themselves in the mirror."

"Except you're outsiders by choice," I said. "You don't have to be sailing the high seas. You chose to become pirates. I didn't choose to be an outcast."

He offered a demure smile. "If you think I chose this, you weren't properly listening."

I felt the warmth rush to my cheeks. "The world has changed while you've been hiding on the high seas, Captain. You might find it more receptive to you now."

He leaned back against his black lacquer chair. "I've got no interest in it. I'm set in my ways now. This is the life for me."

I stifled a yawn. "Too much wine," I said quickly. "The storytelling has been superb."

"We can accommodate you. In fact, I'll offer you my stateroom. It's time to take the helm for a bit anyway. I'll steer a course for Yellowstone." He frowned. "Although it sounds as though that's no longer your destination."

"No, it isn't," I said.

He scraped back his chair. "We can take you as far as Mexico. I'm afraid the rest will be up to you."

"No need, Captain," London said. "A few hours of sleep and we'll be out of your hair. You won't even need to sail to shore."

He stared at her intently. "Is this the magic you spoke of earlier?"

London nodded.

"I should very much like to see it."

I fell asleep quickly but there was no rest in it. I found myself back in the nightmare that had plagued me in Lancaster. The erupting volcano with its flame-colored lava and carrion overhead.

I studied the bird's silhouette. The exceptionally wide wingspan. As it dipped closer, I noted its black and white coloring. The bird seemed to taunt me, waiting to swoop down and claim my flesh once I perished.

I woke up with a start. "It's a condor," I blurted to the darkness. "An Andean condor."

London turned to face me. "Are you having another nightmare?"

"Not this time. Well, yes, but I think my subconscious has been trying to tell me something, only I wasn't listening." I'd been too distracted by the dramatic landscape and the life-or-death situations. "I think it's trying to tell me the location of the dagger."

London folded her hands underneath her cheek. "I'm not doubting you, but you started having these nightmares before we even knew about the dagger. Are you sure you're not making connections that aren't there?"

"No, I'm not sure, but I trust my gut." And it stood to reason that one of us might have a connection to the dagger given the prophecy.

"Did you actually see the dagger?"

"No." I pictured the bird again. "But that condor is significant. I feel it in my bones. I've never seen a real one, only in books."

She offered a small smile. "That's because you can only find them in one region."

"Exactly. That has to mean something."

London pressed her lips together. "Even if you're right, there are five calderas that fall into condor territory. Cerro Guacha, Cerro Galán, Vilama, La Pacana, and Pastos Grandes. Can you remember of any other significant features from your dream?"

I flipped onto my back and sighed. "I wish. It was all

magma and doomsday. There were mountains, but that could be anywhere. If not for the condor, it could've been Yellowstone."

London froze. "Say that again."

I frowned. "It could've been Yellowstone?"

"Right, except we know that's incorrect." She smacked her hand on the mattress. "But only one caldera has ever been referred to as Yellowstone's Southern Sister."

I stared at her. "I'm not the trivia champion that you are. You'll have to enlighten me."

"Vilama. Let's roll the dice on Vilama."

Once again, I was reminded how good it was to have a partner in this adventure. I didn't know how I would've made it this far without London. Truth be told, I wouldn't have. I'd either be dead or still in captivity. I owed her my life.

"Do you like being a knight?" I asked. "Part of a group?"

"They're more than my group. They're my family. Kami's like a sister to me. I'd die for them."

"It seems you'd die for me, too, and I'm not even one of you."

She rolled to a seated position. "You are, Britt. You most definitely are."

I wasn't comfortable with the emotions her response elicited. As someone who'd been cast out, it was difficult to accept there were others in the world who might welcome me. I swallowed the discomfort and chose to focus on the task ahead.

"What do you think? Can you get us there or is the destination not specific enough?"

"I'll do my best but no promises for accuracy."

"Just don't portal us directly into a monster pit. That's all I ask."

"I'll need a few supplies."

I stood and stretched. "I'm sure the captain will be more than happy to provide them."

"I can't believe a vampire as old as he is doubts magic. It seems impossible that he wouldn't have encountered any in all this time."

"Just because he doesn't believe in it doesn't mean he hasn't encountered it directly."

"True. At least there's no chance of him having us arrested for practicing without a license."

"The upside of vampire pirates."

Within the hour London had everything she needed to access her magic, and Captain Presley had earned a front row seat to the performance.

"Whatever you do, don't come after us," I said. "It isn't safe."

The captain held up his jeweled fingers. "You don't need to tell me twice. I've heard enough stories about South America to never even venture as far as Mexico."

"But you said you'd sail us as far as Mexico," I reminded him.

He lifted his chin. "And I would have." He waved a hand. "But this is far more convenient."

I was touched.

London signaled for me to join her in the circle. "We're doing this one a little differently. I keep trying to perfect my craft."

The captain rubbed his hands together. "How exciting for you." His face grew pinched. "Oh, before I forget! Erik, the gifts for our witches!"

Erik strode up the steps to the starboard bow carrying a large, folded cloth. He unfurled the purple fabric to reveal a set of throwing knives and a pile of rope.

"Don't forget the bedroll," the captain said.

Erik turned as a crew member tossed him a bedroll. He passed it into the circle.

"We can only spare one," the captain said. "You'll have to share."

I stared at the bounty in the circle with us. "I feel like we looted you."

The captain seemed fine with the outcome. "It was bound to happen eventually."

"What's the rope for?" I asked.

"It isn't rope. It's a ladder. In case you need to climb down into the caldera. I have no idea how these things work. I'm shooting in the dark here." The captain offered a helpless shrug.

"We use them over the side of the ship," Erik added.

I offered London one of the knives and folded the cloth. "Thank you, really. You've been more than kind."

London centered herself. "Are you ready to witness magic in the flesh?"

Erik clapped his hands in anticipation.

"It was nice meeting you," I said. "Maybe we'll meet again someday."

Erik handed his partner the black guitar. "Perhaps you can serenade them as they make their exit."

The last thing I heard was the opening chords of Only Fools Rush In.

"You're a real comedian," I said into the void.

Chapter Five

We arrived in the middle of a mountain as a storm brewed around us.

London shot me an apologetic look. "It's not an exact science."

"It's okay. I didn't expect to land directly in front of the dagger." Life was never that easy, at least not for me.

"What do you think? Up or down?"

It was hard to decide. I closed my eyes and let my instincts guide me. "Up," I finally said.

"Are you sure there isn't a bit of clairvoyance in your blood?" she asked as we started to climb.

"It's possible, but either way it's faint enough that it barely counts as a verifiable skill. I'm better off calling it my gut."

I adjusted the bedroll strapped to my back. It added a layer of warmth that I welcomed as a gust of cold wind whipped through me. Thoughts of the dagger pushed aside any discomfort. We needed to be the first one to find it. Our lives depended on it.

The wind seemed to be gaining strength the higher we

climbed, as though willing us to seek our fortune elsewhere. Lightning flashed ahead of us now, followed quickly by a thunderclap. Terrific. Now we were walking straight into the storm. I was hoping we might've arrived at the tail end of it.

London stopped walking. She bent over to rest her hands on her thighs. "Do I need to point out the weather is starting to turn?"

"Just another lucky break," I said sarcastically.

"If I knew the dagger was at the summit, I'd try to portal us there."

But we didn't know. The dagger could be anywhere along the mountainside and if we portaled higher, we risked missing it. We also risked portaling ourselves to another caldera.

The next gust of wind carried a loud and jarring sound. London turned her head to look at me. "Did you hear that?"

Nodding, I twisted to look behind us. Nothing.

We stood in silence and listened.

Another bolt of lightning. Another roll of thunder.

And then—*hee haw*.

London cracked a smile. "Is that a donkey?"

It wouldn't be completely out of the question. Donkeys brayed and they were perfectly content to wander mountainsides, monster-infested though they were.

We continued our trek up the mountain. Maybe the storm would end as quickly as it began. The rain hadn't started. There could be a deluge and then dry as a bone again.

London pointed to the right up ahead. "I think that might be a cave. We can take shelter there until the storm passes."

We made it inside just as fat drops of rain began to

pound the caldera. The cave was steeped in black, and it was impossible to tell at a glance how deep it was.

"Should we explore the cave?" I asked. For all we knew, there was information about the dagger etched on the walls.

"I think we should take a sign from the universe and rest."

I was torn between searching for clues and doing the sensible thing.

"I wish I had Babe with me," London said with a heavy sigh.

"Is that one of your animal companions."

"No, my axe."

I laughed. "You named your axe?"

"I name all my weapons." She cast me a curious look. "You don't?"

"It never occurred to me."

"Well, you should definitely start."

"Why? Do you think they work better when you name them? They're inanimate, you know."

"Words have power. Names have power." She picked up a sharp rock and began to carve her name into the wall. "You know this, though. If you didn't, you'd still use your surname."

I flinched. "I don't use Miller because I don't want to be associated with those people in any way."

"Exactly. The name Miller has power. Britt the Bloody has power. The Demon of House Duncan has power." She closed her eyes. "By the gods, I miss Callan. When this is over, I'm not leaving his side for a solid six months."

"Okay, you've convinced me. When I'm reunited with my weapons, I'll name them all."

Thunder boomed outside. Apparently, the storm had decided to stick around.

"Come on. That's a definite sign we should rest." London wiped the cave floor with the bottom of her boot. "Not the most scenic spot."

"I've slept in worse places."

"Same. One of us should probably take watch."

She was right. A storm might drive two witches to take shelter, but that didn't mean monsters wouldn't be on the prowl. This area had been hard hit by the Great Eruption and abandoned by civilization as a result, allowing the monsters to thrive and multiply.

"I'm not too tired," I said. "I don't mind first watch."

London unrolled the bedroll and curled into a ball with her back against the wall. "What's the worst place you ever slept?"

"It was in the Southern Territories. I was surveilling a vampire over the course of a couple days. He didn't go anywhere without a buddy, so it was hard to isolate him. Anyway, I ended up camping out in a dumpster behind the restaurant he owned. It was the only way to stay out of sight and disguise my scent."

She laughed. "Delightful. Mine was one of the tunnels in Britannia City. There must've been a monster at the opposite end because I awoke from a deep sleep to find dozens of rats trampling me to get away."

"I'm assuming New York rats are as big as Britannia City rats."

London held her hands out to show me their size. Yep. Like a pack of feral hogs.

"That had to hurt," I said.

"Oh, it did. I had a broken rib and bruises all over my body, but at least no monster."

"You win," I told her. "Now, go to sleep."

She closed her eyes and I swiveled to face the mouth

of the cave. The storm raged outside and, once again, I heard the braying sound. It was louder now—closer. Maybe the donkey was coming to its senses and seeking shelter. Part of me hoped it would. A donkey might come in handy.

Rain pounded the ground outside the cave. I heard a noise behind me and craned my neck to see London pulling herself to her feet.

"You're up already? Go back to sleep. You get at least another hour."

A guttural sound emanated from her throat.

"London?" I rose to my feet. "Is something wrong?"

As I focused on her face in the darkness, I noticed the intensity of her expression. Something wasn't quite right.

"London?" I asked quietly.

Blood-red eyes stared back at me. Those weren't the gray eyes of my companion.

She pounced.

"London, you're possessed!" I wasn't sure if she could hear me, but I had to try to reach her any way I could.

She snarled and tried to bite my shoulder. I clocked her cheek and backed away. I didn't want to hurt her. On the other hand, letting her eat me didn't seem like a brilliant plan either.

She snapped her teeth and advanced again. Whatever had control of her seemed intent on biting me. As long as it didn't figure out what else London was capable of, I could manage. Hopefully.

I focused on London's body and attempted to form a connection with her blood. Although I didn't want to violate her in this way, I didn't see a choice.

I felt the magic snap into place and let the tendrils slither through her blood. I eased the flow and saw the moment the inhabitant felt the change. The red eyes widened and then narrowed.

London hissed and charged again. This time she knocked me flat against the jagged wall. The back of my head slammed against a rock and my jaw rattled. Thankfully the impact didn't render me unconscious and my connection to her blood remained intact. Her teeth scraped my skin. The upside of no fangs. I shoved her backward and made another attempt at slowing the blood. I had to be careful not to overdo it and kill her.

The beast within her raged at me. Either London was more powerful than I realized or the monster in possession of her was. I couldn't remember the last time I'd met this much resistance when taking control of someone's blood. Even a dragon had proven easier.

I concentrated harder and *pushed.* If I could force the blood...

There.

London slumped to the floor in a heap. Third time's the charm, it seemed. A loud, braying sound filled the cave, piercing my ears momentarily before receding with a whoosh.

A heavy silence descended upon the cave. The pressure practically forced me to a seated position.

I released my control of the dhampir. "London?"

Her eyes opened. No more red.

She pressed a hand to her throat. "What happened?"

"A minor possession. It's gone now. I had to slow your blood, but it seemed to do the trick."

"I'm so sorry. Did I hurt you?"

I crouched beside her. "Not as much as I hurt you."

She rubbed her cheek. "Now that you mention it...It'll heal quickly. One of the perks of being half vampire." She turned to look at me, her face radiating sincerity. "I can't apologize enough."

"It's okay. I knew it wasn't you."

"It was an Anchancho," she said, her voice hoarse.

"What is that?"

"An evil spirit. I should've realized it was stalking us when we heard the braying sound, but it's been so long since I learned about them..." She trailed off.

"Your mother?"

She nodded. "They tend to dwell on mountain peaks and are active during storms."

"They possess people and then what?"

"It wanted your blood. They're not vampires, though. Different species. They don't even have their own bodies."

"Do you think there are more?"

"Hard to know, but I think we should get moving."

The storm outside had grown quiet, so I agreed.

"I wish you could've rested as well."

I smiled. "I'm not sure I'd call what you did resting."

"True, but I think I managed a solid hour. We can try again later."

"It's no problem. I'd rather get the dagger and get out of here." There was no rest for the wicked, anyway. I may not have been inhabited by an evil spirit, but I had plenty of inner demons that plagued me. It was a good thing the spirit possessed London instead of me or I fear I might've killed her.

Reluctantly we resumed our climb. The earth was softer now thanks to the downpour, which didn't make things any easier. Just slippery.

"If you're going to go to all the trouble of crafting a dagger from the obsidian of a supervolcano, why leave it there?" I complained as we trudged up the mountainside. "Why not transport it somewhere more accessible?"

"It was probably intended for sacrifices at this particular caldera. They had no reason to move it."

"Then it must be kept somewhere special. We're not going to find it embedded in a random stone we pass."

I was relieved when we finally reached the top of the caldera.

"It looks like we're standing on a giant ammonite," London observed.

I peered over the edge at the spiraling rock. I shuddered picturing the monsters that would have risen from its center during the Great Eruption. "I wonder how it's changed since the first time it erupted."

"I didn't study them in depth, but I bet there's a book at the library that could tell us."

I smiled. "How about I leave that exciting research to you?" My idea of pleasure reading was more along the lines of children's books.

"There's an amazing library in Britannia City. You should visit and I can show it to you. They know me there."

"Why does that not surprise me?"

She skirted a boulder. "I'm starting to feel the tiniest bit resentful that this third witch is out there living her life without the slightest exertion on her part."

"Who knows? Maybe her life is harder than ours has been. Maybe the universe is cutting her some slack."

"If the universe wanted to cut her slack, it wouldn't make her part of a doomsday prophecy."

"It's only a doomsday prophecy if you're a full-blooded vampire," I pointed out. "Or if you don't want Trinity Group in charge."

"We really are between a rock and a hard place." She stopped to observe her current position. "Literally."

From where we currently stood, there was no obvious path down the other side. "Let's walk along the perimeter. Maybe we'll see a path."

London stared at the center below. "I think I see water at the bottom."

I followed her gaze. Tendrils of steam emanated from the body of water. "How hot do you think it is?"

"Hot enough that I don't recommend swimming."

The odds were good that we wouldn't need to travel that far anyway. The dagger was likely hidden somewhere between here and the bottom layer.

"Any instincts as to where this dagger might be?" London asked.

"It's here. That's as much as I know right now." I felt a tugging sensation in my gut, like there was an invisible cord that connected me to the dagger.

We continued walking along the perimeter. The top of the caldera was eerily quiet. No wind. No ambient noise. My skin pricked with anticipation.

"We're close," London said, echoing my thoughts.

"To the dagger?"

"To something important."

"How can you tell?"

"Because every hair on the back of my neck is standing at attention right now."

I smiled. "Now who's the clairvoyant one?"

London was the first to spot a carving in the stone wall. "Look at this."

A sunken-cheeked figure grimaced at us.

"I think it's meant to be a god," she said, "but I don't know which one."

The figure was followed by a series of runes chiseled into the stone. "Recognize any of these?" I asked.

London examined the carvings. "I think we're on the right track."

"What makes you say that?"

She touched the image of a funky, backward 'Z.' "Because this rune means 'sun.'" She tapped the next rune of two triangles kissing. "And this one means 'day.' It can signify beginnings and endings."

I stopped at the sculpted figure of a skeleton seated on a cup. "This is it."

"What's with the skeleton on the loo? He's all bones. He doesn't have a bladder anymore."

"It's not a toilet. It's a cup. Together they symbolize mortality." I tossed her a triumphant look. "Finally, I know something you don't."

London studied the carving with interest. "It's a warning."

Of course it was. When would there be a welcome mat with a chilled bottle of champagne and a platter of lobster tail?

"Now that we have a clearer idea of our destination, is there any chance you can portal us to the dagger now?"

London held up her hands, palms facing the caldera. "Can you feel that?"

I closed my eyes and focused. A current of magical energy rippled ahead of us. "I take that as a no." I glanced down at the red stone clasped around my neck. "What about the amulet?"

"We're not dealing with coven magic this time. This place is designed to protect the dagger. The energy feels... primordial. Captain Presley was right about the challenges. The only way to the end is through them."

Not the answer I wanted to hear. I inhaled sharply. "Fine. Are you ready to do it the old-fashioned way?"

Her answer came in the form of a single step forward. Nothing happened. No death rattle. No earthquake. No magical attack.

I joined her past the carving. "In order to save ourselves from certain death, we're facing certain death. You get that, right?"

"The irony isn't lost on me. Still, I'd rather choose to face death than be at someone else's mercy."

I gripped her hand in mine. "Same."

Together we began our descent.

Chapter Six

I strained to listen to our surroundings as we descended the caldera. There was no telling when we might encounter another monster like the Anchancho.

I paused at the sound of rushing water. Although we'd glimpsed steaming water at the center of the caldera, this was closer. "Do you hear that?"

London smirked. "It's like we're back in Central Park."

She and I had encountered multiple raging rivers in a hidden realm amidst the city park.

Sure enough, we arrived at a torrent of water that seemed to circle the entire caldera.

"Looks like a ring of Saturn, except water instead of rocks," London observed.

I pivoted toward her. "Now you know about space, too?"

"What? It's general knowledge."

"Not to me."

"Then consider your time with me a learning opportunity."

I laughed. "Oh, believe me. I do." I observed the river.

Based on the steam rising from the surface, swimming wasn't an option here either. "How do you propose we get across? If you dip so much as a toe in there, you'll lose it."

"I have basic elemental magic," London said thoughtfully.

"Do you think you might be able to freeze a sliver of the river, enough to get us across?"

Hesitation rippled across her features. "The water is so hot, and I have no idea how deep it runs. It would be extremely risky. If it cracked while we were on it, we'd be screwed." She pointed to her right. "Like those guys."

I'd been so focused on the river, I hadn't noticed the bones. They were scattered along the bank in a variety of shapes and sizes.

"You think all of these belonged to people seeking the dagger?"

London shrugged. "Hard to know. Could be monsters."

I wasn't fond of either scenario.

London plucked a bone from the ground. "Looks like a femur. What do you think?"

I stared at the bone, an idea forming. "Let's gather them up, as many as we can find."

London frowned. "I don't think now is the time for a proper burial."

"I don't want to bury them. I want to use them." I motioned to the river. "To build a bridge."

"A bridge of bones?" London pondered the width of the river.

I slipped the bedroll from my pack and unrolled to find the folded fabric from the pirates. "We have rope and knives. We can cut the rope into pieces and use them to tie the bones together."

"Why not just throw the ladder across?"

I pondered the suggestion. "How's your knowledge of science?"

She seemed to understand my thought process. "We might give ourselves enough time to cross before the rope dissolves."

"The bones would be solid, less give. We can't risk the rope dipping into the water when we put weight on it, or we might lose the rope *and* a foot. The water won't melt the bones. It's the perfect solution, as long as we maintain our balance."

London watched the steam rise from the water and dissipate. "What about the return journey? There's no way the bridge will last long enough to cross it on the way back. We'll be lucky if we both make it across now."

"We'll cross that bridge when we come to it?" I cringed. "Sorry. Had to be said."

"Did it, though?" London began collecting bones while I started slicing apart the rope ladder to use the pieces as ties.

I examined the opposing riverbank. "Which do you like better for the anchor on the other side? That stump or the boulder?"

London surveyed the offerings. "The boulder's better except it's too wide. It'll be hard to get the rope around it to secure it."

"So, the stump?" I couldn't tell from this distance which type of tree it had once been, but any stump that had survived lava and monsters had to be sturdy enough for our purposes.

Her shoulders slumped. "I don't see a better option. You'll have to get the loop right the first time. If you miss, we'll lose the whole bridge."

"No pressure."

"This is going to take some time," I said, as I began the tedious task of tying bones together.

London added another bone to her growing collection. "Whatever it takes, right? Unless you see a condor that wants to fly us across, we're on our own."

We worked diligently to create the bridge. Once London had amassed enough pieces, she joined me in creating a patchwork of bones and rope.

I crafted a loop at the end that I hoped was the right fit for the stump on the other side. As long as it wasn't too small, we could make it work.

I twirled it in the air like a cowgirl and London used her modicum of air magic to guide the rope to its target. I held my breath as the loop landed around the base of the stump.

"Achievement unlocked," London said and patted my back.

We affixed our end of the bridge to an obliging boulder that was large enough to act as an anchor but not so large that it required too much rope. We stretched the bridge taut so that it hovered about an inch above the steaming water.

"Who wants to go first?" I asked.

"I think we should cross one at a time, so we don't stress it too much."

I agreed and offered to go first. The bones were smooth, which presented a slight problem when trying to climb over them. Halfway across my foot slipped and I managed to snap it up before it touched the steaming water.

"Take your time," London called. "No rush."

Once my heartbeat calmed, I continued my journey. Some of the ropes were already beginning to fray, whether from the stress or the heat I wasn't sure. I hoped they held for London.

I exhaled loudly as I landed on the other side. I felt like throwing up. I turned to cheer London on.

She moved as nimbly as a cat. It was clear she'd been thinking about her technique while I was taking my chances. She made it to the other side and jumped daintily to the ground.

"Go team." I surmised the bridge. "I really hope it holds up for the return journey." I fully recognized there were a lot of assumptions packed into that statement.

We scanned the area ahead. There were slabs of stone too tall to scale and too close together to squeeze between.

"I don't see a way through," London said. "Do you think there's a path further along?"

As we advanced, the earth trembled in response. It seemed we were about to find out.

The stone wall ahead of us separated and then smashed together.

"I'm going to take a stab in the dark and say we need to pass between them," I said.

The stone slabs split apart and rammed together again. It happened far too quickly for their size and weight. Then again, that was probably the point.

"Which one of us is faster, do you think?" I queried.

"Doesn't matter. We both need to get through."

True. "You have vampire speed."

She licked her lips as she observed the crashing pieces. "That I do." She cut a glance at me. "What if one of us gets through and the other gets stuck out here?"

I smiled. "I like your sunny optimism that the other one doesn't get smashed to bits." My spine tingled at the sound of the caldera wall crashing together again.

"I have extra strength," London said with her gaze pinned to the obstacle.

"What do you suggest? Trying to keep them apart until I get past?"

She turned to look at me. "No. I carry you on my back."

I frowned. "Won't that slow you down?"

"Might not be enough to matter."

It was the 'might' that stuck in my head. "Then we'd both get crushed."

London released a breath. "I suppose so."

"You said you have elemental magic, right?"

"Nothing that would help with this. My elemental magic isn't powerful enough." Her eyes lit up. "But I do have another skill that could help us." She zeroed in on my face. "This is sort of a strange one. Are you ready?"

"More like intrigued. Go on."

London took a few steps back and concentrated.

"Is your skin vibrating?" I asked.

She shushed me. I watched in disbelief as she peeled off a layer of herself to create a second London.

"What?" I couldn't even form the rest of a question. "What just happened?" I asked again.

"This will help us."

"What is this, exactly?"

"They're versions of me."

"Okay. Won't these other versions of you die?"

"It's not a problem, as long as the real me doesn't get crushed. They're forms of magic."

I watched in fascination as London peeled more versions of herself off her body and formed a line of them.

"I think six will be enough."

Each one was identical to the original. Amazing.

"They only need to hold the walls back long enough to allow us passage," London explained. "Then their job is done."

"And what happens if they survive? They rejoin you?"

"They just dissolve into the ether."

I regarded her with a mixture of awe and envy. "I'm really starting to feel like I got the short end of the magic stick."

London looked at me. "Believe me. You don't want to trade places, not with past me anyway."

Nobody in their right mind would want to trade places with past me either.

"Are you ready?" she asked.

I shook my arms and legs to loosen my muscles. "Ready."

We moved as close as we could get to the crashing walls. The other versions of London gathered ahead of us, three on each side.

"Now!" London commanded.

The versions jumped into the gap as the stones separated and held their respective sides at bay.

London dashed through the narrow gap with me hot on her heels. The stones slammed together just as I passed through and managed to snag the bedroll.

"I'm stuck," I called.

London pivoted to face me. "Hold on." She maneuvered behind me and detached the bedroll.

"A small price to pay," I said. I craned my neck for a look at the sealed wall. There was no sign of any Londons. "They didn't make it, huh?"

An icy wind blew past us and my arms instinctively flew around my body in a protective gesture.

"It's a hot magma lake down there," I complained. "Where's the cold coming from?"

"I think it's the next part of the test."

The temperature continued to decrease to the point

where my teeth started to chatter. The cold air felt capable of ripping the skin right off my body.

"I...can't...walk," London said. Her mouth barely moved as she spoke.

We huddled together in an effort to stay warm.

"Fire...magic," I said.

London's teeth clacked together in my ear. "Try." She closed her eyes and I noticed the icicle forming on her lashes.

We had to act now.

London tried to move her hand. "Can't," she chattered.

It was becoming difficult to think. I knew there was another possibility. Something to stave off the cold.

Blood.

I used blood magic to warm myself from the inside out and then turned my attention to London. It took a few tries before I was able to reach her blood. My head was still fuzzy and the connection kept slipping. I touched her arm in an effort to stay focused.

London widened her mouth to stretch her jaw. "It's getting better."

The words sounded slightly warped, but I understood them. I continued to increase the blood flow until London's breath stopped coming out in white puffs and the icicles melted from her lashes.

The wind picked up again as we progressed, and I started to worry that I'd have to tap into my blood magic again. I didn't want to exhaust myself before we arrived at the final challenge.

A powerful gust blew back my hair and forced my eyelids closed. This wind wasn't icy, though, only strong. When I opened my eyes, however, I realized it was worse than I thought.

Much worse.

A dozen knives sliced through the air toward us. The sharp blades whistled as they sailed past us—thankfully without striking either one of us.

"Talk about an ill wind," London cracked. For a brief moment, it was like having Liam beside me. As much as I missed my friend, I was glad he wasn't on this particular journey. London's skills were more useful than werewolf brawn.

Another dozen knives hurtled toward us. London cartwheeled to the side to avoid making contact while I dove to the ground.

"How many knives do you think there are?" she called, loudly enough to be heard over the roar of the wind.

"If we're lucky, we'll find out." I peered at the horizon, trying to determine their starting point.

London dodged behind a black boulder and whistled for me to join her. I waited for the next lag and bolted for the large rock. It was tall enough to protect us if we crouched low enough.

"This one's obsidian," I remarked.

"And?"

"And we can move it with us. Use it as a shield."

"Good thinking," London said.

Together we moved the boulder in front of us to deflect the onslaught of knives. The fact that it was obsidian meant it was lighter yet stronger. A regular boulder would've been much harder to move.

Slowly, we pushed our way forward. Blades bounced off our makeshift shield and landed on the ground around us as we progressed. We pushed the boulder until we reached the next ring of the caldera.

The flight of knives stopped.

I poked out my head from behind the obsidian shield and observed a set of rocky steps leading down to the next pathway. There was no sign of clear and present danger.

I dashed to the steps first and hurried to the lower ring with London right behind me. I swiveled right to left and then I saw it up ahead. An enormous rock with the handle of a dagger visible. The blade appeared to be embedded in the stone.

Before I could get a closer look, a hulking figure moved to stand between us and our final destination. Towering over us, the monster revealed not one, but two sets of sharp fangs that extended from one side of its head to the other. It looked as though someone had used a blade to carve two lines across the monster's face. Its massive arms were covered in dark green scales and its legs were thick enough to rival an elephant's.

"Is this a 'you' problem or a 'me' problem?" London asked.

"I think it's an 'us' problem," I replied, although I knew what she meant. My attempt to tap into its blood and form a connection was met with resistance. Either the creature didn't have blood or it had the ability to fend off attacks like mine. I'd never seen anything like it before and certainly couldn't identify it.

"Do you think it's a crossroads demon?" London asked.

She and I had encountered one during our journey to deliver a god of darkness for judgment.

The monster tipped back its giant head and groaned in dismay. "Do I look like a crossroads demon to you? They're covered in poisonous spikes and ugly as sin." The monster held out a bulging arm. "These scales are luminous in the right light. No spikes."

I couldn't tell which mouth was doing the talking. They both seemed to move.

"Never mind this guy," London said. "You get the dagger. I'll hold him off."

I turned to look at the dagger. I doubted it would be as simple as pulling the blade from a slot. This monster could kill London while I was busy trying to figure out how to extract the dagger.

"No, we stick together."

"I'm feeling stereotyped," the monster said. "What if I don't want to fight you?"

London eyed him closely. "Then what are you doing here? Isn't it your job to stop us from getting the dagger?"

The creature shrugged his massive shoulders. "I'm a guardian, sure, but you made it this far. That proves you're worthy."

I stared at him in disbelief. "So you're just going to let us waltz up and take the dagger?"

He chuckled. "I'm sure I don't need to tell you it's not that simple." He motioned to an indented boulder off to the left. "I'm happy to sit and watch. I can't offer any pointers, that kind of interference is forbidden, but I'll cheer you on." He held out a hand. "The name's Trevor, by the way. My parents used to call me Little T, but they're dead now so..." He trailed off awkwardly.

"I'd hate to see Big T," I murmured as I shook his hand.

"I have to admit, I'll be thrilled if you succeed. I've grown tired of hanging out here. I'd like to travel. See the world."

"How did you end up here?"

"Got tricked into it. They needed a replacement for the last guardian who died. What can I say? I was naive, but the agreement was valid, so I can't leave unless and until that dagger is removed. Them's the rules." He held up his hands in acquiescence.

"And you really don't have to try to stop us?" London asked.

Trevor pulled a face. "Technically, I guess I'm supposed to discourage you, but it's been so long, like I can't even tell you a number, that's how long it's been." He waved a hand toward the middle of the caldera. "It's a nice waterfront view and all, but it gets a little boring century after century. So few visitors."

I shot him a curious look. "We're not the first?"

"Nah, there've been a handful." He paused. "Okay, that's not strictly true. Nobody's made it all the way to me before. I've seen them get as far as the chopping blocks." He cringed. "Not a pretty sight, as I'm sure you can imagine."

I edged closer to the dagger. "What do you know about the dagger?"

"Nothing I can share. I had to sign an NDA as part of the job."

"Who's going to enforce an ancient NDA?" London asked.

"Oh, you'd be surprised. It's a mystical contract, so the punishment would be instant and automatic." He sliced a finger across his neck. "If they'd drafted it better, then I'd be forced to fight you for your final trial, but there were a couple loopholes in the document that I'll happily exploit."

Their loss was our gain.

Trevor stepped aside, allowing London and I to approach the fruit of our labors.

Folding her arms, London gave me a pointed look. "What was that about the dagger not being embedded in stone?"

"Okay, but this is more Excalibur-style."

"You think only someone worthy can extract the dagger?"

I held up my hands. "That rules me out."

We both turned to look at Trevor, who pretended to zip both sets of lips.

"I'll try first." London warmed up her wrist before gripping the handle of the dagger.

"Want me to count to three?" I offered.

She tossed me a look. "I don't need a deadline." She drew a deep breath and pulled.

Nothing happened.

"Ouch. That's gotta hurt. Your pride, I mean," Trevor said.

London ignored him. "It could be warded. We should try to use magic."

We both studied the dagger from multiple angles. "What kind of magic?" I finally asked.

"I don't know. Let me try a few spells."

Trevor wrapped his hands around one knee. "What do you ladies intend to do with the dagger? Christmas present?"

"We plan to keep a group of witches and wizards from using it to kill us," I said.

Trevor nodded from the sidelines. "Offense is the best defense, I always say."

London tried using air magic to loosen it. Then earth magic to loosen the rock. Nothing helped. The dagger refused to budge.

"It's mocking us now," London remarked.

I threw up my hands. "I'm useless since there's no blood in a stone or a dagger." I lacked London's inherent vampire strength.

We seemed to hit on the same idea at the same time. It

made sense that blood was the key to removing it. The dagger was sacrificial. Its entire existence was for the purpose of extracting blood.

I used one of Captain Presley's throwing knives to draw a line across my palm. Blood dripped onto the handle of the dagger.

"Try to take it now," London urged.

I curled my fingers around the dagger and tugged. It slid out of its prison with ease.

Trevor rose to his feet and started to clap. "Congratulations. Well deserved, truly. It's been a pleasure..." He wasn't able to finish his sentence. He simply disappeared.

I gazed at the dagger in my hand. "Do you think this means the original creators of the dagger had blood magic like me?"

"At least one of them did. Maybe that's why the sacrifices fell out of favor. Once they lost the witch or wizard with blood magic, nobody was left who could wield the dagger."

"It seems unfair that the witch who can withdraw it is also destined to be murdered by it."

"Not destined," she reminded me firmly. "That's why we're here, remember? To take control of our fate."

I nodded. London was right. I wasn't going to let Olis or anyone else decide when and how I get to die.

"Now that we have the dagger, what are the chances of using portal magic to get out of here?" The fact that Trevor disappeared was a good sign.

London closed her eyes and I watched as her skin shone with silver light. She opened her eyes and smiled. "We are go for launch."

"Too bad we couldn't do this sooner."

I studied the obsidian dagger. It was surprisingly plain

for a dagger with so much power. "Now we have to figure out how to destroy it."

And that could take time. We'd spent the little time we had simply trying to find the dagger. We hadn't gotten as far as destroying it.

"We need to keep it somewhere safe in the meantime," I continued. "Somewhere no one else could find it."

London smiled broadly. "I know just the place."

Chapter Seven

London left me at the bottom of the caldera while she returned to her pocket dimension with the dagger. She reappeared a few minutes later empty-handed.

"Are you sure it's safe there?" I asked, although the question sounded ridiculous even to my own ears. It was a pocket dimension of her own creation. What were the odds anyone would stumble upon it?

London squeezed my arm in a comforting gesture. "Trust me. I have experience hiding important objects there."

"That's a handy skill to have. Is it wrong to be a smidge jealous?"

"My magic wouldn't have helped rid my body of an evil spirit. I think we both have coveted magic." Her hands glowed silver and she absently wiped them on the sides of her pants. "Where do you think we should go for research? Britannia City has an excellent library."

I smiled. "So I've heard. I think we might be better off starting with oral historians and avoid any obvious places of knowledge." It would be too challenging for us to research in public places when we were being hunted. If I were Trinity Group, I'd have witches and wizards stationed at every library and house of knowledge in the world right now. They had to know we'd be researching the dagger, even if they didn't know it was already in our possession.

"Know any promising oral historians?" London asked. "My mother would've been a good resource." She sighed. "Gods, she would've loved this."

"I don't think she would've loved the part where her daughter was hunted for a sacrifice."

"No, but she always knew I'd be in danger. It's why she hid the truth about my identity in the first place."

"And then there was my parents, learning the truth about my magic and handing me over to the coven to be cast out." I gave a rueful shake of my head.

"They didn't deserve you," London said.

"No, they didn't." I frowned. "I know your mother isn't here to help us, but can you think of anyone she might've mentioned with historical knowledge, preferably with a magical specialty?"

"My mother was a witch, so she definitely knew..." Her eyes rounded. "Yes! There's one on your continent, in fact. More than one, actually. A powerful tribe of magicians called Kewawkgu."

I'd never heard of them. "You think they might have the kind of knowledge we need? And they won't betray us to anyone at Trinity Group?"

"They're magicians, not wizards, so I highly doubt they'll be involved with Trinity Group."

It made sense. Historically magicians and wizards viewed each other as magical rivals.

"They're also quite insular. I doubt they mix with outsiders much at all."

They sounded like a promising option, except for one detail. "Whatever we tell them, I still don't think we should reveal the purpose of the dagger."

London angled her head. "You think their desire to bring back the sun will be stronger than their desire to help us?"

"At this point I don't think we can trust anybody with the truth. Where can we find them?"

"The Ottawa River Valley. The tribe has been there for centuries."

Perfect. Nobody would think to look for us there. "Can you portal us?"

She looked at her hands, still glowing silver. "Yes, I think so, or at least get us within striking distance."

"What happens if you don't use magic often enough? You'll explode?"

She grimaced. "More or less."

Between portals and the dagger extraction, London had been using a lot of magic lately. Her system had to be more powerful than I realized if that wasn't enough to suppress the silver glow.

I stared at her hands in awe. "How did you manage to hide that silver glow from everyone?" It was a dead give-away that she was a dhampir.

"It's been a constant source of stress."

"I'm sure." I couldn't imagine the pressure. It had been easier for me to hide my magic. Strangers didn't have a way of knowing unless I used it on them and if that happened, you were as good as dead.

"Did King Callan know what you were from the start?" I asked.

She shook her head. "Nor my banner. It took a long time for me to trust anyone with my secret, but Callan has worked to change the laws in our land and remove the death sentence for my kind."

"He must really love you."

"He loves me, but he also sees that it's the right thing to do."

"Another honorable vampire. Who knew? If only there were more."

"We don't simply need more honorable vampires. We need more honor amongst all species."

"Amen, sister."

The Ottawa River Valley was located slightly northwest of Montreal. It was surprisingly lush for a sunless land. No doubt the Kewawkgu tribe played a role in the area's continued vitality. I wondered whether they had House approval to use magic. On the other hand, the land was so remote from civilization, it was possible vampires either didn't know or didn't care.

"Do we know anything about these magicians?" I asked as we walked along the banks of the Ottawa River. "Are they prone to violence?"

"I don't think so."

I glanced ahead, searching for signs of life. "How close do you think we are to the village?"

"Three-quarters of a mile, as the crow flies," a voice said.

We turned abruptly. A slender man stood behind us wearing a brown cloak and well-worn sandals. His head was so bald that it practically shone in the darkness.

"Apologies. I didn't mean to frighten you. My name is Geoffrey LaPierre."

"I'm Britt and this is London. We're searching for the Kewawkgu."

"And so you've found us." He placed his hands in prayer form and bowed. "What business have you with our tribe?"

"We'd like to speak to your historians."

His face took on a bemused quality. "Historians? I must admit, that's the first time I've intercepted such a request."

"We seek knowledge about an ancient artifact," London said. "We think someone in your tribe might be able to offer information on the subject."

His head bobbed. "We do have many with knowledge that extends back to before the Great Eruption."

"We'd love to speak with them," I said.

He held up a finger. "First, a test. I serve as a guardian. We have them posted throughout the region to protect our village."

London groaned. "We've had our share of tests this week."

Geoffrey grinned. "I can tell. Still, it's a requirement for passage to the village."

She lifted her gaze to his, her shoulders weary. "All right then. How do we prove we're not a threat?"

"You let me peek inside your head."

London recoiled sharply. "Absolutely not."

"I have to agree with London. That's too much of a violation."

"We need to be certain you mean us no harm," Geoffrey explained. "We can't rely on your word."

"Isn't there another form of magic you can use that doesn't involve rummaging through someone's private thoughts?" she demanded.

Geoffrey rubbed the back of his neck. "Well, I have an alternate method that I suppose is less intrusive."

"Good. Let's go with that," I said.

He gave us a sly look. "What have you two got to hide?"

"Nothing to do with you," London said.

I knew she was concerned about her secret. It was impossible to know how the tribe would react to the presence of a dhampir.

Geoffrey flexed his fingers. "I'm going to lay a hand on your shoulder and feel your energy. That will give me the basics without the specifics. How does that suit you?"

"Like an aura reading," I said.

"Very similar, except I don't see colors or anything. Just feel a sensation. Now, this won't hurt a bit." He started with me and grimaced. "Ouch. You've got baggage to unpack." He quickly moved to London. "Lots of complex emotions, but no desire to harm us." He patted London's shoulder. "Come on, I'll escort you to the village."

"And what would you have done if we'd posed a threat?" I asked as we continued along the riverbank.

He seemed surprised by the question. "Killed you, of course. We take no chances here. There's too much at stake."

Our surroundings grew more abundant as we walked.

"Ottawa was once a large, thriving city," he explained. "That changed after the Great Eruption."

I slapped a hand to my chest. "Something changed after the Great Eruption? Shocker."

He didn't smile. "Vampires swept the region. If not for the foresight of our tribe, we would've been wiped out."

"They never returned to force you to swear fealty to them?" London asked.

He shook his head. "They can't control what they cannot see."

"What do you mean?" I asked. "What can't they see?"

He spread his arms wide. "All of this land is invisible to them. If vampires were to pass, it would appear as nothing more than a barren wasteland of no interest to them. Even this part of the river would appear dry."

"But we found you," I countered.

"You are not vampires." His gaze shifted to rest on London. "Your witch blood counteracts the spell."

I glanced sideways at London. "You weren't kidding about their power." It took a lot of magical juice to keep an entire community hidden from view. "I'm surprised House sensors haven't picked up strong pulses of magic from this part of the continent."

"We haven't encountered a sensor in decades," he said, puffing his chest. "And when we have, we've always managed to send them away as ignorant as they arrived."

"We don't want to leave ignorant," I told him. "Not when we're here for knowledge."

"Knowledge is a worthier cause than subjugation. We'd be more than happy to assist you if we can." Geoffrey guided us to the village entrance which was marked by two mighty oak trees. "Katarina will take you from here."

A young woman appeared beyond the trees and beckoned us forward. Her brown cloak was identical to Geoffrey's except for a patch in the shape of a ladybug.

"Katarina, our visitors would like to see one of our historians. Anyone available?"

The young woman nodded with enthusiasm. "I'll bring them to see Paige."

"Excellent. You're in good hands. Best of luck with your quest." He bowed and retreated from the trees.

Katarina's smile was pleasant and soothing. "Paige is in the eastern garden."

The eastern garden was just past the tranquility center and the healing hall. We garnered a few curious looks on our way to seek wisdom.

"Miss Paige." Katarina spoke with her head lowered. "You have visitors."

Paige stood amidst a dizzying array of flowers, holding a watering can. "Thank you, Katarina."

The young woman withdrew from the garden.

"It's almost as good as your pocket dimension," I whispered to London. I'd never seen a garden like this before in the real world. There were roses, lavender, heather, clematis.

London inhaled deeply. "It smells like heaven."

Paige set the watering can on the ground and approached us. Her plump face was lined with age and her white head retained only a few brown strands.

"Where on earth have you two come from?"

"Long story," I said. "But we're here for one of yours, not one of ours."

She cocked her head to the side, intrigued. "Oh? What kind of story?"

"Have you ever heard of the Blade of Fire?" I asked.

Paige's brow furrowed as she contemplated the question. "Blade of Fire...Is it made from obsidian?"

"That's the one," London chimed in.

She looked from London to me. "You seek this dagger?"

"We seek information about it," I clarified. It wasn't a complete lie. "We'd like to know how to destroy it."

"Why would you want to destroy an ancient artifact?"

"So it can never be used to hurt anyone ever again,"

London said. We were skating dangerously close to the full truth.

"And you've decided that we might possess such knowledge here?" Paige motioned toward the village. "Why not go to a library or somewhere like the Atheneum for this kind of information?"

"Too risky," London replied. "There are powerful people who wish to use the dagger and want to prevent its destruction. We couldn't seek the information in an obvious place."

"I see." She stared at us for another prolonged moment, as though taking the measure of us. "You must be famished after your long journey. If my senses are correct, I smell my Pandora's cooking." She vacated the garden. "We thought my daughter might've been born without access to magic until she was old enough to boil a pot of water." The hint of smile passed her lips. "Then we discovered her true talent."

"I wish that was my talent," London grumbled. "When left to my own devices, it's all watery soup with barely any nutrients."

We cut between two small, wooden buildings and arrived at the pale blue door of a stone cottage.

Paige opened the door without knocking. "Hello, dearest. I've brought along visitors."

The aroma of freshly baked bread set my mouth watering. Magic, indeed.

The kitchen was basic—an oven, stovetop, and a wooden block formed the countertop. Pots and pans hung from the ceiling. A middle-aged woman bustled back and forth. She shared her mother's full cheeks and other cherub-like features.

"Pandora, I'd like you to meet our guests." Paige motioned for us to introduce ourselves.

"I'm Britt and this is London." I breathed in the scent of spices from the pots. "And this is divine."

Pandora smiled. "Thank you, that's kind of you to say. I've been working on a new recipe for when my husband returns from his supply journey."

"And we're the lucky test subjects." Paige began collecting plates and cutlery and marched them to the farmhouse table in the small dining area.

"It's a vegetable stew," Pandora called in an apologetic tone. "Meat isn't plentiful, as I'm sure you know. Our tribe has adapted to the change over time. We grow our own vegetables. Fruit is somewhat more difficult in this region, even with magic, but we experiment."

"There's a rationing schedule for those who wish to partake in meat. As it happens, this is my week." Paige set out the plates. "I believe it's pheasant, so I don't feel like I've missed out."

My stomach gurgled.

She turned to smile at me. "If it appeals to you, you're more than welcome to my portion."

Dear gods. I was literally taking food out of their mouths. "I'll be fine with the stew, but I appreciate the offer."

London nudged me gently with her elbow. *Honor*, she mouthed.

They're honorable people. Got it.

"Please, sit," Pandora urged as she carried over the pot of stew and set it in the middle of the table.

London and I sat across from Pandora and her mother.

"How do you keep the garden so bountiful? And the village hidden? The amount of magic you must produce is staggering." I seemed to be chewing as fast as I spoke.

"Magicians have a reputation for having less potent

magic than witches such as yourselves, but the truth is we've learned to work together for the collective good in a way that makes all this quite simple to maintain." Paige tore off a piece of bread and popped it into her mouth. "I taste the rosemary, Pandora. It's magnificent." A small moan escaped her as she chewed.

"Now I have to see what the fuss is about." London ripped off another piece from the loaf and her expression was nothing short of euphoric. "You have a true gift, Pandora."

The woman grinned with pride. "It's nice to hear. I went through many years thinking I had nothing to offer the tribe at all. I was real worried I'd be..."

"Cast out?" I interrupted.

Pandora looked appalled. "Cast out? Because I had no magic?"

"No, never," Paige said, equally shocked by the suggestion. "We don't cast anyone out unless they've committed an unspeakable crime."

"And when was the last time that happened?" London asked.

"Not in living memory," Paige said.

Given the whiteness of her hair, it had been a very long time, indeed. It seemed the type of magic wasn't the only difference between the Lancaster coven and the Kewawkgu tribe.

I let the spices of the stew coat my tongue. I'd never tasted anything as bold or as interesting. "This is phenomenal."

"You're both making me blush." Pandora waved us off. "You must stop."

"So, what is it the two of you can do?" Paige asked, drawing her napkin across her chin to catch flecks of stew.

"I'm always curious when I meet a witch. You're such a varied species."

I decided to come clean and gauge their reaction. "I'm a blood witch."

Paige gazed at me with unbridled curiosity. "Are you really? I've heard of such magic, but I thought it might be a myth."

"Not a myth." No one screamed at me for possessing dirty magic or cowered in fright. I liked this tribe. Too bad they'd hidden themselves away from the rest of the world.

"Fascinating," Pandora said. "Is that what you can do as well, London?"

London seemed less confident about revealing herself. "I possess a smorgasbord of magic."

"A smorgasbord." Pandora smiled, revealing a gap between her two front teeth. "Now you're speaking my language."

"I can do a bit of elemental. A bit of...other stuff." She offered a nonchalant shrug. "I'm a Knight of Boudica by trade. I'm primarily based in Britannia City."

The magicians registered shock.

"And you've come all this way?" Paige asked. "You really are in dire need of answers, aren't you?" Her brown eyes seemed to look straight into my soul. "May I see the dagger in question?"

"What makes you think we have it?" I asked.

Paige drank the water from her cup. "I understand it must be difficult to trust when the world has made trusting difficult for you, but I'm only a historian of the Kewawkgu. We keep to ourselves and have no interest in House politics." Her gaze landed on me. "Or those of covens."

Without warning, the front door burst open and a trio of children swarmed the room.

"Joshua, you're not due for another hour," Pandora said, rising from the table.

"Lessons stopped early today on account of a Yeti sighting."

"A Yeti?" London repeated.

"We get them in our region every now and again," Paige said. "They tend to travel solo and don't pose much of a threat. They're mainly interested in our crops."

"Joshua, Maddie, Dakota, please welcome our visitors, Britt and London." Pandora bustled into the kitchen to collect more plates for the children.

"Pleased to meet you," Joshua said. He studied me. "You look like you've been through the wars."

Paige gasped. "Joshua, what a thing to say. Where are your manners?"

Pandora clucked her tongue. "Your father won't be pleased to hear how you spoke to two very powerful witches in our home."

Joshua assessed us. "How powerful are we talking?"

"Sit down and eat," Pandora ordered. She slapped stew on his plate and continued to serve the other two children, who squeezed their chairs together at the table. I remembered breaking bread with families during my early years. I'd envied their camaraderie and easy rapport. Even when they were exchanging jibes and pestering each other, there'd been a sense of affection present.

"Why are you here?" Maddie asked.

"We're looking for information from your grandmother," I said. "We were told she might be able to help us destroy an ancient dagger."

Joshua's eyes practically bulged out of his head. "Can I see it?"

"We don't have it with us," London said. "We do have it, though, to answer your question, Paige."

She nodded somberly. "Where did you get it?"

"South America," I said, omitting our trek to acquire it. "The Vilama caldera."

"No way," Joshua said, his mouth stuffed with stew. "You went to one of the supervolcanoes in South America?"

"We did," I said. "It was a matter of necessity."

"I want to be an explorer, but my mom and dad say I can't leave the village." His expression turned sour. "No one does unless it's for a supply run or a hunt."

"Has it been well preserved?" Paige asked. "I imagine it has. Obsidian is impressive."

"It's made from obsidian?" Joshua asked in awe.

"We have to find a way to destroy it," I said.

Her son leaned forward intently, resting his elbows on the table. "Or what? Natural disasters? Floods? Earthquakes?"

"We don't know the details," I said, which was true. We had no idea the repercussions that the sun's return would trigger. Hotter temperatures. Melted ice caps. Floods. Vampires might not be the only casualty.

He twisted to regard his mother. "Natural disasters might work in our favor."

His mother whacked him on the back of the head. "Quiet, Joshua. We're not interested in your scorched earth approach to diplomacy."

Glowering at us, Joshua fell silent.

Paige set down her fork. "Based on what I know, I'd estimate the dagger to be at least two ages old, maybe more."

"Two ages?" I echoed. "Is that your term for a century?"

She chuckled. "Oh, you sweet thing."

"The age we now live in was not the first," Pandora interjected with less amusement than her mother.

"Everybody knows that," Joshua interjected.

Pandora shot him a warning glance and he shoved another forkful of stew into his mouth.

"You mean the age before the Great Eruption?" I asked.

"I mean the six ages prior to now," Paige said.

Beside me, London choked on her water. "Six?" she croaked.

Paige nodded. "Each of those ages had its own sun, its own history."

"Its own sun? Different from the one that's up there now?" I pointed skyward, a futile gesture I realized. We only had it on faith there was any sun at all.

"How does that even work? There's only one sun in our solar system. The Great Eruption blocked it," London said.

Paige shrugged. "Perhaps. Perhaps not."

"Are you saying that sun is gone?" I asked.

"I am not playing the role of scientist. I am merely sharing with you historical views that differ from what you've learned. That there have been suns in past ages... The implication being that there can be another sun and this sun—this new age—will usher vampires back to the shadows where they've dwelled in previous world ages before this one."

"The literal dawn of a new era," I said, more to myself. How did that tie into the prophecy? Would my death bring forth a new sun? Francesca seemed to think it would force open the clouds and allow daylight to penetrate the atmosphere. A whole new sun—that was a different scenario all together.

"You won't destroy it," a voice said, as smooth as butter. A man swaggered into the cottage. His cheeks were ruddy, and his shirt was only half tucked into his pants.

"No one invited you, Malcolm," Paige said.

"I didn't even hear the door," Pandora murmured.

"Seems you should include me in a conversation like this one." He slapped both hands on the table. "That's some stew you've got there. Kudos to the chef."

Paige folded her arms. "Never mind. Maybe if you were sober, we would've thought it wise to include you."

Malcolm's face split into a wide grin. "Paige, you know I'm every bit as wise drunk as I am sober." He turned that mischievous grin to me. "Why don't you introduce me to our beautiful guests?"

Paige shot a helpless look at her Pandora.

"We've got this, Malcolm. Go sleep it off," Pandora said.

Malcolm straightened and held up his hands. "No need to get belligerent."

"You said we *won't* destroy it," I told him. "Are you saying it's because we can't?"

He flashed another mischievous grin. "I'm not a part of this conversation, remember?" He leered at me. "Too bad. I would've enjoyed talking to you, sweetness." He backed out of the cottage until the darkness swallowed him.

"Charming," London murmured.

"Who is he?" I asked.

"Malcolm has the Sight," Paige said with a weary sigh. "It's a burden to him, though. He doesn't cope well with it, so he drinks."

"How does his ability work?" I asked. "Can he see the future?"

"Glimpses," Paige said. "He usually shuts down before it shows him more. He suffers from headaches that all the herbs in the world can't seem to cure."

"Does he ever see prophecies?" London asked.

"He's no seer," Joshua interrupted with a derisive snort. "He's lucky if he predicts what dinner will be."

Pandora smacked the back of his head again. "Go make yourself useful elsewhere before I assign you latrine duty for the week."

She didn't need to tell him twice. He pushed back his chair and scrambled from the table.

"Would you mind if I spoke to Malcolm?" I asked.

Mother and daughter exchanged wary glances.

"He's not what you'd call a gentleman," Paige said. "Likes to say things to make women uncomfortable."

"I can handle myself."

Paige gave me a begrudging nod. "Suit yourself. You'll likely find him in the barn. That's where he prefers to drink."

London made a move to join me, but I put up a hand. "You stay here. If I'm not back in fifteen minutes, come find me."

The two of us together would no doubt intimidate Malcolm and I wanted him to let his guard down. A magician with the Sight and a huge chip on his shoulder wasn't to be underestimated.

Sure enough, I found Malcolm seated in a haystack outside the barn. He clutched a bottle in his hand. He smirked when he noticed me.

"Decided you liked the look of me, eh?"

"No, I decided you might be useful, even drunk."

He glanced down at his crotch. "Not sure Mr. Winky would agree with you."

I rolled my eyes. "Not the kind of useful I mean."

"Too bad." He tipped back the bottle and drank.

"They tell me you have the Sight."

"Three-eyed magician. That's me." He tossed the empty bottle on the ground and peered at me. "You came a long way for information."

I lowered myself to his level so that I wasn't towering over him. "What does that tell you?"

"You're desperate."

I nodded. "You could say that."

Malcolm leaned forward. "What's in it for me?"

"The pride of using your talent for something productive instead of winning at cards?"

"Can't win at cards." He shrugged. "Not allowed to play anymore."

"You're the only one in the tribe with this particular gift, I take it?" I settled beside him on the haystack.

He scowled. "Don't call it a gift. I hate that."

"It gives you headaches."

"Awful ones where I feel like someone took a sledgehammer to my temples. Sometimes I think Athena herself is about to emerge from my head in full armor."

"None of the tonics are strong enough to help?"

He shook his head. "My mother spent years trying to concoct a mixture that helped."

"She gave up?"

He offered a rueful smile. "She died."

"I'm sorry." I couldn't imagine how terrible the pain must be if an entire tribe of magicians couldn't ease it.

"You suffer, too," he said. It wasn't a question.

"You've seen it?"

"Not like a picture of your past or anything. I felt pain and suffering when I looked at you."

"Are you like Geoffrey?"

He moaned loudly. "Great gods above, no. It's because I

suppress my ability. It still finds a way to send me messages. Stubborn fool."

"London and I have both fought similar battles."

"That's the other one's name? London?"

"And I'm Britt." I offered my hand. "Pleased to meet you, Malcolm."

He shook it reluctantly. "Does it get easier?" he asked.

"When you stop resisting, yes."

"If I stop resisting, I'm pretty sure it'll kill me." A hint of sadness appeared in his eyes. Malcolm's gift was torturing him.

"When's the last time you let it happen without fighting it?"

His jaw clenched. "Five years ago."

Very specific. "What happened?"

"I watched my sister die in my head and then I watched her die in real time." He tossed a handful of hay into the air. "What's the point of having the Sight if I can't do anything about what I see?"

"You tried to save her."

"I went straight to the river as soon as the vision passed. I saw everything, knew where to go and what was about to happen." He closed his eyes. "And I still failed."

I placed a hand on his arm. "Malcolm, having the Sight doesn't mean you're responsible for what actually happens."

His face crumpled in anguish. "Do you think fate is sealed? Inevitable? What I see must come to pass?"

"Not necessarily, but you shouldn't blame yourself for what you can't control."

His jaw set. "My grandmother saw the rise of the Fallen. Noko tried to warn people long before the Eternal Night began, but no one listened except our tribe."

"She had visions like you?" I asked.

"She had the Sight, but her ability manifested differently. Noko saw omens and portends." Malcolm tipped his head back to stare at the dark expanse above us. "She could read the sky like a book and knew when a catastrophe was imminent."

"And she foretold the Great Eruption?"

His face grew pained as he nodded. "And then had to live through it. She was only a young girl at the time. She awoke one night to the sound of wailing voices, the harbingers of impending death. The next day was an earthquake and reports of active volcanoes."

"And eventually the Great Eruption."

He nodded gravely. "That's when our tribe took notice."

I offered a wry smile. "Hard not to notice when the whole world is on fire."

"Noko recognized this cataclysmic event as the drumroll before vampires took center stage. She urged the tribe to take steps to protect itself."

"Which is how this place ended up hidden from the world."

"Noko saved us from extinction. Once darkness fell, other people waited for the sun to rise. They believed the ash would eventually clear and light would return to earth."

"But your tribe didn't wait," I prompted.

"No, they respected Noko. The omens she saw terrified them. Our magicians would return here with reports of terrible monsters and annihilated villages. Eventually they stopped leaving all together. It was too dangerous."

"Did your grandmother ever have any visions about the return of the sun?" I asked.

Malcolm's soft gaze met mine. "Can't say I know anything about that, other than the story of ages you heard from Paige. She's a smart one, Paige." He wagged a finger at me. "But don't tell her I told you. I like to play adversary with her. She's feisty for her age."

"Any visions of the Blade of Fire being destroyed?"

He pulled a face. "Nothing springs to mind. Sorry."

"How are you two getting along?" London asked, stepping into the artificial light.

"We're good," I said. "Aren't we, Malcolm?"

A snore erupted from Malcolm.

London laughed. "He must've found you captivating."

I gazed at the sleeping figure against the haystack. "He thinks everything he sees will inevitably come to pass." I paused. "Do you believe the prophecy will come to pass no matter what?"

London leaned against the doorframe. "I think no single path is set in stone. There's more than one option for us, just as there's more than one option for the return of the sun."

"Then why do you think Trinity Group is so intent on this one prophecy?"

"Because the game pieces are already on the board," she said. "Think about it. They know two of three witches. They're actively seeking the third. It's simply the fastest route to get what they want."

"Then once we destroy the dagger, we have to remove more pieces from the board."

She watched me expectantly. "What do you suggest? We find the third witch before they do?"

"There's an easier option."

"What? We go into hiding for the rest of our lives? Not an option. I'm a Knight of Boudica. I spent most of my life hiding my identity. I don't hide anymore. I fight."

As much as I understood her position, I disagreed. "It's too dangerous to stay together. If we separate, we make things harder for them. They can't play the game without the pieces."

"Together we're stronger."

I gave an adamant shake of my head. "Together, we offer ourselves up on a platter. The best way to save ourselves is to stay apart."

London seemed torn. "Which one of us destroys the dagger?"

"I'll do it. You go back to King Callan. Stay as far away from me as possible."

London gripped my hands. "You want me to leave you here?"

"Yes, bring me the dagger and then portal yourself home."

Malcolm's eyes popped open. "She'll be fine. She's heading to Connecticut next."

I looked at him. "I am?"

London squinted. "She is?"

"Starlight Casino. Red hair and freckles." He belched. "Don't worry. You'll see each other again," he said in a faraway voice.

"You promise?" London asked.

Malcolm's eyes fluttered closed again. "I don't control it, remember? I'm just the messenger."

Maybe he was right and we would see each other again, but would it be when we were tied to our funeral pyre? The devil was in the details.

As much as I hated to leave my friend, I knew it was the right thing to do for both of us. "Good luck, London. I'll be rooting for you."

She seemed to choke on her words. "I'll be rooting for you, too, Britt."

Chapter Eight

London delivered the dagger to me and then portaled home, leaving me at the edge of the Kewawkgu village.

"Look out for Yetis!" Joshua called, waving furiously.

They'd been kind enough to provide me with a map and supplies for the journey to Connecticut. Pandora had also tucked a loaf of the rosemary bread in the pack, for which I was eternally grateful. The best gift the tribe gave me, however, was a motorcycle. No helmet and the rusted bike wasn't in the best shape, but even if it got me as far as upstate New York it'd be worth it.

Paige told me which ferry to take across the river so that I wouldn't have to present any kind of identification. Apparently, there was one for smugglers that was sometimes raided, but she thought my chances were good since there'd been a raid last week. Arguably I could whip out my girlfriend-of-the-king credentials, but I was trying to maintain a low profile so that Trinity Group didn't catch wind of my location.

I made it into New York without incident and

continued along all the backroads. If I maintained a steady pace and kept my stops to a minimum, I calculated I could arrive at the casino in about seven hours. I still had no idea what I expected to find there, but Malcolm seemed certain that was where I needed to go next.

I was so focused on navigating the bumps in the road that I missed the tripwire. I flipped up and over. The bike skidded across the dirt, and I landed on my back with a searing pain emanating from my tailbone.

"Nice bike," a gruff voice said. "We'll take it."

"I don't think so." I tried to get up, but the back of my head throbbed and dropped back to the ground.

"Hancock, tie her arms and legs."

"Oh, no. Not again." One kidnapping this month was quite enough. I kicked at Hancock who approached me with a ball of twine.

"What is it?" someone asked.

"*It* is a witch," I called to the darkness. I looked at Hancock. "Tell them."

"She's a witch," Hancock called back with trepidation. "She doesn't want to be tied up."

"Nobody wants to be tied up." The voice paused. "Well, maybe on special occasions. Anyways, just do it."

I peered at a line of silhouettes in the background. "You've got the bike. What do you need me for?"

"Don't know yet. Maybe you've got magic we could use."

I sat up and dusted off my pants. "Magic is prohibited."

A ripple of laughter followed my statement. "Yeah, sure," the same gruff voice said. "This is pack land, missy. If we say you can do magic on our behalf, you can do it."

I thought I sensed wolves, although with his curly hair

and skittish nature, Hancock struck me as more of a werepoodle.

Hancock held out the twine. "May I?"

I released a weary sigh. I'd show some restraint. See what they wanted and then I'd kick their asses if I disliked the answer.

"No need for twine. Easier for you if I walk anyway."

The group escorted me to tiny cabin set apart from a cluster of other buildings. "The VIP suite, I presume."

One of the wolves shoved me forward and I tripped over the threshold.

"Yo, easy," the gruff voice said. "Big Boss won't like it if she thinks we roughed up the merchandise."

"I am not merchandise. I'm a guest in your luxury accommodations." Nothing could've been further from the truth. The cabin was devoid of furniture, save a single chair on its side across the room. No windows. No sign of a toilet even.

Hancock set the chair upright. "Would you mind taking a seat?"

The wolves pressed closer and forced me toward the chair. It seemed I'd have to endure an intimate moment with twine after all. Although I could've taken a few of them at once, there were too many to fight, especially if they started shifting. The one with the gruff voice was over six-and-a-half feet tall with a chest made out of concrete.

Hancock bound my wrists behind and then my ankles.

"Big Boss is coming," one of the wolves muttered and moved aside.

"Does that make you Little Boss?" I asked the large wolf.

Without responding, he turned toward the doorway

with a hangdog expression. "Hey, we weren't gonna start without you or anything, Big Boss. Pinky swear."

Big Boss turned out to be a woman half the size of the large wolf. Even more importantly, she turned out to be someone I knew.

"Hey, Meghan."

She strode forward with the same confidence I recalled from our encounter in Virginia. "Of all the dens in all the world, you had to come strolling into mine."

Except Meghan wasn't part of any pack when I met her. She lived alone, not in a den. She'd been married to a vampire who'd been one of my victims during my assassination days.

"How did you end up in this den of thieves?"

"I'll ask the questions." Her face looked hard enough to chisel and I wondered whether she'd changed her mind about me since the last time we spoke, although Twila had mentioned Meghan's helpful presence in D.C. Maybe something terrible had happened to send her on this path.

What was worse than an assassin killing her husband?

Meghan pivoted to face the pack. "Leave us alone for a few minutes. I know how she fights. Dirty."

"She can't fight tied up like that," Hancock said.

Meghan folded her arms. "Shows what you know. This witch can kill you just by looking at you."

"Then why hasn't she?" he asked.

"Because I want to talk to Meghan, not kill her," I interjected.

Meghan pointed to the door. "Out."

One by one the werewolves reluctantly vacated the room, except the big guy. He positioned himself by the door like a bouncer committed to keeping people in rather than out.

"You, too, Digit."

"I'm your second."

"I don't need a second for this."

"Aren't you the beta if she's the alpha?" I asked.

She turned to look at me. "We don't use those antiquated terms here. It's one of the changes I implemented when I agreed to take a leadership role." She flicked a glance at Digit. "Go," she barked.

Once the door clicked close behind him, Meghan turned back to me with a sheepish grin. "I am so sorry, but I had to put on a good show. They're generally pretty cool, but you never know."

I relaxed slightly. "Can you untie me now? Hancock scratched the hell out of my wrists with that twine."

Crouching beside me, she released the bindings. I stretched my arms and wiggled my hands. "What's the protocol? Do we hug?"

"I don't think physical contact is necessary."

"Got it." We stared at each other awkwardly for a split second. "How did you end up here? Twila said you spent time in D.C. helping out."

"I came up this way to start fresh," she explained. "A cousin of mine is in the pack and he invited me to visit. I liked the area and the wolves seemed friendly, so I decided to stay."

I arched an eyebrow. "And then decided to take charge?"

She splayed her hands. "There was an opening."

"And your second didn't want to be the first? He has alpha written all over him."

"This might surprise you, but Digit likes to be submissive."

My eyebrows inched up. "So, you and he are..."

Her gaze dropped to the floor. "We're a thing. It's still new, so we're trying not to put labels on it."

"Meghan, I'm so happy for you."

"Thanks." Dropping to her bottom, she leaned against the wall. "Truth be told, I'd been feeling adrift. After fighting beside you against the Pey, I realized it felt good to be part of a group. I was tired of being on my own."

I understood the sentiment. "And you decided to find a group of your own?"

"I've never been much of a joiner, but I thought it was time to mix things up. Figured if I didn't like it that I could always change course again."

"But you like the pack?"

"I do." She smiled. "Weird, right?"

"Not really." I couldn't picture Liam here, but Meghan seemed settled. Content.

Her gaze lowered. "I'm sorry I didn't return your calls. I know you meant well. I thought about it, if that means anything to you."

"You don't have to be sorry. We don't need to be friends."

"Part of me wanted to reach out." She sighed. "I just wasn't sure whether it was your guilt that made you contact me, or whether you genuinely wanted the friendship."

Now it was my turn to sigh. I felt like I was expelling all the negative emotions that had been building inside me since Lancaster. "Honestly, Meghan, I'm not convinced I'm cut out for friendship."

She nudged me with an elbow. "Seems to me you had plenty of them."

"And where are they now? In danger, thanks to me."

"Who's in danger?"

"Me. London—you don't know her. Liam. George."

Meghan stiffened. "What happened? Tell me."

I shook my head. "I don't even know for sure. As soon as I finish this task, I need to get back to the city and find them."

"What's the task?"

"It's probably best if you don't know. I wouldn't want to endanger you too."

"That's your fear talking. Come on, Britt. The witch I know is more resilient than that." She cracked a smile. "Are you hungry? We've got plenty."

"That's not a sentence I hear very often." Not from any group except vampires.

"The pack has a system. The fact that we're based in the middle of nowhere helps."

"How are you finding enough food to satisfy an entire pack?" Werewolves were the biggest eaters of any species I knew. Their impressive metabolism demanded sustenance.

"There's a magically infused forest twenty miles from here. We send a hunting party every two weeks or so."

"You would think the keepers of the forest would know when to expect the next hunting party."

"They killed one of them early on to set an example."

I winced. "And they didn't send for reinforcements or House assistance?"

She shrugged. "If they did, nothing ever came of it. Like I said, that's the beauty of being in the middle of nowhere." She licked her lips. "Which begs the question—why are *you* in the middle of nowhere?"

I told her about the kidnapping, the prophecy, and the dagger.

Meghan laughed when I described the carnage in Lancaster. "Those assholes deserved it."

"I don't know. I have a strange relationship with the word 'deserve.'"

She nodded. "I get it, but they got what was coming to them. What's the plan now?"

"Destroy the dagger. Find out where Liam and George are."

"What makes you think they aren't where you left them?"

"Because they would've found me by now. They would've pulled out all the stops." I nudged her. "Somebody would've tracked you down. Roger, maybe."

"Must be nice to have concerned friends. I showed up here and nobody knows. Nobody cares."

I looked her in the eye. "That's not true, Meghan. I cared. It would also help if you passed along your new phone number to people." I caught the hint of a smile.

She smacked her head. "Twila."

I nodded.

"I'll call her. Do you know how to destroy the dagger?"

"No clue. That's what I'm hoping to learn at the Starlight Casino."

"Who sent you there?"

"A magician with the Sight."

She grinned. "You meet all kinds, don't you?" Her smile melted away and I suddenly felt uncomfortable.

"What's wrong?"

"I just remembered something." She rested the back of her head against the wall. "Ugh. I hate being the bearer of bad news."

Icy fingernails dragged down my spine. "What bad news?" What could be worse than everything I just said?

"I heard talk recently. I'm not sure how legit the intel is, though."

"Another prophecy starring yours truly?" I was only half joking.

"No, this is about your...King Alaric."

My breathing hitched. "What about him?"

"He's hosting some big event soon. The Great Gathering. Know anything about it?"

"No. What is it?"

"He's invited all the royal vampire leaders from around the world to the House August compound in the city. He wants to talk about reform." She licked her lips. "I don't know who, but somebody's planning a takedown."

"A takedown? Like a coup?"

"Bigger than a coup. A massacre. Think about it. He'll have royal vampires from every House there. All in one convenient place for killing."

I suddenly felt sick to my stomach. "Where did you hear this?"

"One of our scouts is friendly with a witch in a nearby town." She hesitated. "When I said I considered calling you earlier, that was the reason. I wanted to tell you in case...I wouldn't want you to go through what I did."

Her remark slammed into my chest. I was the one who'd put her through that particular hell when I murdered her husband. The fact that she wanted me of all people to avoid the same pain spoke volumes about her character.

I tried to catch her gaze, but she refused to look at me. "Thank you, Meghan. You have no idea what that means to me."

"That's all I know. I wish I could tell you more."

"You can tell me the name of the witch and where I can find her. I'd like to ask her a few questions."

"I don't know her name, but I can take you to Dean. He's the one who told us."

My pulse raced. If Alaric was in trouble, I had to get word to him. The more information I could wrangle first, though, the better.

Meghan accompanied me to a cabin at the edge of the enclave. The door was painted a bright shade of yellow. She pounded on it with her fist.

"Hey, lazy bones, open up. I need to talk to you."

I shot her a quizzical look and she shrugged in response.

"What? He's lazy."

The door opened and a slender man stared back at us. He stood about six feet with medium brown hair and a full beard. His gaze darted from Meghan to me.

"Why'd you bring her here?"

"Her name is Britt," Meghan said. "And she needs information from you."

Dragging me by the hand, she pushed past him into the cabin. For a lazy bones, the interior was surprisingly well-kept and tidy.

"Why would I tell her anything?" Dean asked in a low voice. "I heard she consorts with the enemy."

Meghan drew closer to him with her chin positioned at a defiant angle. "She consorts with me."

His lips widened to a smirk. "Oh, does she now?"

"Not like that, you idiot." She punched him in the gut. "Tell her what your witch told you."

Dean cast a hesitant look in my direction. "I wasn't expecting an interrogation. I was only sharing intel."

"I'm not the Inquisitor," I assured him. "I'd like to speak to the witch and get more information. There are people I care about in that compound. If there's an attack planned, I need to warn them, or at least get them out in time." I pictured George and Liam imprisoned somewhere while an attack raged around them. They'd be sitting ducks.

"Who cares if a bunch of vampires bite the dust? That's good for all of us."

"Tell her," Meghan insisted. "She saved this whole pack from the Pey without you even realizing your butts were on the line."

A woman emerged from an adjacent room wearing nothing except a short silk robe. "How about I tell you myself?"

"Go back to the bedroom, Renee," he growled.

"You don't tell me what to do, you overgrown Schnauzer," she snapped. The witch waltzed up to me, giving me the once-over. "You want to know what I heard, do you?"

"I think I've made that clear." She didn't strike me as a card-carrying member of Trinity Group. "Who told you about the attack?"

"My cousin. He's always mixed up in some kind of drama. He was an anarchist until he moved to New York City and started hanging out with wizards he met in a bar."

"That made him stop being an anarchist?" I asked.

"It made him become a magic supremacist. Suddenly witches and wizards should rule everything because they're more powerful and, therefore, destined to rule." Renee rolled her eyes. "I don't know why everything is all or nothing with him. Just give me a quiet cabin with a hot bod and enough food to eat and I'm a happy camper." She smacked Dean's backside. "Right, babe?"

"Can you tell me any details about the plot? Day, time, what the attack will involve?" I'd take any sliver of information at this point.

"All I know is it'll happen during this big gathering, which starts tomorrow if memory serves." She cast a sidelong look at Dean. "Is tomorrow the thirteenth? Yeah, it starts tomorrow and it's a three-day event or something, so I'm not sure when the attack itself will take place."

"Are they planning to storm the compound with magic? Poison everyone's goblets of blood?" My mind was rife with ideas, each one more unpleasant than the last.

"My cousin said it's a two-prong attack, whatever that means. He seemed real pleased, like he thought it up himself."

She snorted. "Newsflash. He didn't. I love the guy, but the wizard couldn't tie his shoelaces with a spell. In fact, I'm pretty sure he uses Velcro."

The revelation was unsettling to say the least. Alaric was in danger, and if Liam and George were being held somewhere in the compound by Olis, they were at risk too. I had to save them, even if that meant saving every royal vampire in attendance.

"Do you happen to know the name of the group organizing the attack?" I asked, not that I really needed to ask. I only sought confirmation.

Renee bit her lip, thinking. "He might've mentioned their name one time when he first started hanging out with them, but I don't remember. I tend to tune him out when he starts rambling." She opened and closed her fingers in imitation of his mouth.

It wasn't as much information as I'd hoped, but it was better than nothing. "Thanks, Renee. I appreciate you telling me."

Dean frowned at her. "Seriously. Why save vampires?"

"Because I don't want these other losers in charge of anything either. Anybody who thinks they're superior to the rest of us isn't anybody I want in power."

He snaked an arm along her waist. "Don't you think I'm superior, baby? That's what you told me last night."

She leaned into him. "I didn't use the word superior."

He grinned down at her. "Sure you did."

"I need to get to New York and warn Alaric myself. That's my best bet."

Meghan's nose scrunched in protest. "You just told me everybody is hunting you, but you think that's your best?"

"I'll have time to think on my way to Connecticut."

"Sounds like you're in need of an escort."

I waved her off. "Absolutely not, Meghan. You're finally happy somewhere. I wouldn't dream of dragging you away now."

"So I'll come back here afterward. No big deal. I like the open road."

I contemplated her offer. It wouldn't be the worst thing in the world to have a companion with fighting skills.

"Then you'll have to return here on your own."

She smiled broadly. "How do you think I got here the first time?"

Meghan could handle herself. I knew that. But still. "I don't want anything to happen to you because of me." Anything else, that is.

"Are you coddling me? Britt the Bloody, that's downright insulting."

I backed off. Meghan was right. I couldn't let my guilt interfere with a welcome offer of assistance. "I would love a companion, especially one who fights like you."

She clapped my back. "There you go. That wasn't so hard now, was it?"

She opened the door to find Digit standing there, along with what seemed like half the pack.

"What's going on, Meghan?" Digit asked. "Why'd you guys come to Dean's?"

"She needed information about that vampire coup we

heard about," Dean volunteered. I could've smacked his gorgeous face.

Meghan gave me a sheepish look. "Remember that part where I said I trusted them?"

"Yes."

She grimaced. "I may have lied. We need to go. Now."

I tried to contain my disappointment. There'd be time for lamentations later—hopefully.

Meghan slammed the door shut between us and locked it. "That will hold them for two seconds."

"Back door," Renee said, pointing.

"Hey, whose side are you on?" Dean asked.

It didn't matter. The cabin was surrounded.

"Hand her over," Digit said. "Let's not do this the hard way. Everybody here likes you and we don't want you to give us a reason to hurt you."

Meghan's eyes blazed with furious indignation. "Like any of you could hurt me. I'd break half your bones before you managed to wrap those baby dill fingers around my neck."

Frowning, he looked at his hands.

"Come on, Meghan," another werewolf said. "You're one of the pack now. That means we're all on the same page."

"Then be on *my* page, Stewart," Meghan shot back. "Britt is my friend and she needs our help."

"I'm not helping anybody whose ultimate goal is to save vamps," Stewart said. "That doesn't align with my core values."

"Your core values involve taking a larger portion of meat when you think no one's looking and sticking your pickle in Niko's girlfriend, so forgive me if I'm not falling over myself to honor them."

Laughter erupted in the crowd.

"What is it with you and pickles?" I whispered.

The pack closed in on us. Waves of tension crashed over me. I could practically smell the testosterone in the air. This wouldn't end well for us.

Two strong arms pushed their way through the crowd. "Did I hear you mention my name?"

"Niko?" I said to Meghan, who nodded.

The wolf closest to him whispered in Niko's ear. His eyes widened and he whipped around, presumably to find Stewart.

"Not now," Digit ordered. "We're in the middle of a situation."

Niko didn't care. The only situation that seemed to matter to him was the one that involved his girlfriend and Stewart.

"Niko, it was only one time, I swear." Stewart held up his hands in a placating gesture.

"One time too many," Niko said. He swung.

Meghan grabbed me by the wrist. "Run!"

Half the pack seemed transfixed by the fight while the other half seemed intent on chasing us. Without London's portal skills, I didn't know how I'd get out of this predicament. I was fast, but I couldn't outrun an entire pack of wolves.

"Where's my bike?"

"No idea," Meghan panted.

I heard the snarling and cracking of bone as they shifted. They'd be faster now. Terrific.

I glanced at Meghan, already ahead of me. Even in her human form, she was fast. She seemed to sense my concern and twisted to observe me. The look of shock on her face spurred me forward. I heard the thunder of paws as the wolves closed the gap between us.

My heart pounded with fear. I couldn't use blood magic on them. There were too many and they were moving too fast.

My foot slipped and I stumbled forward. The toe of my boot snagged on something solid and propelled me head over heels. I heard Meghan cry out as I landed flat on my back. Again. The ground trembled beneath me. Before I could move, Meghan fell on top of me. The ground shifted.

"Shit," Meghan muttered.

The earth opened its gaping maw and swallowed us whole.

Chapter Nine

I looked up to see the trapdoor, or whatever it was, had snapped closed again. Fabulous.

"Are you okay?" I asked. I winced as I tried to straighten my legs. Despite the pain radiating from limb to limb, nothing seemed broken.

"I'll heal quickly enough." Meghan rose to her full height and surveyed the underground cavern. "Where in the hell are we?"

I gave my eyes a moment to adjust. It was much darker down here and that was saying something. "I think it's some sort of tunnel." I felt my way to the nearest wall and ran my hand along the cool stone. "There are markings here."

"Are you sure they aren't just cracks in the stone?"

I pressed my finger into the grooves. "No, it's more than that. There are patterns."

"Can you figure out what they say?"

I traced the pattern and tried to envision them in my mind's eye. "I wish I had a light."

Meghan made a noise. "I totally forgot." A moment

later, a small flame appeared. "Lighter. Digit smokes a pipe before bed and he likes me to light it for him."

"I thought you said he was submissive."

"Acts of service is his love language." She held the flame closer to the wall. "He can kiss that goodbye, the traitor."

"I think he might see things the other way around. You were the one who ran off with their prisoner." I stopped talking when I caught sight of the symbols on the wall. I recognized some of them from the compound. "I think this is an old vampire lair."

Meghan scrutinized the wall. "Are you sure?"

"Pretty sure. I bet there was an enclave here before the Eternal Night." Vampires would've used the tunnels to travel during daylight hours. "What's our closest city?"

"Albany. Why?"

"I bet they'd travel to the city for supplies and then return here."

Meghan sniffed the air. "It smells earthy, like patchouli."

"No blood?"

"Not that I can smell."

Small favors. "Any ideas on how we get out of here?"

She glanced up. "We can't go out the way we came in, so I suggest we follow the tunnel and see where it leads."

"Will the others be able to track us?" I asked.

"They'll lose our scents and break into smaller groups to search the area. I doubt they'll figure it out unless they fall through like we did. The door snapped shut again."

I'd have to rely on Meghan's nose to guide us. My eyesight was relatively useless in the pitch black. The lighter flame wouldn't be enough.

I touched the wall. More carvings.

"Can you tell what they are?" Meghan asked.

I followed one of the grooves and then another. "Symbols. I have a feeling these tunnels were in use for centuries before the Great Eruption." They'd likely fallen into disuse once vampires crawled out from their hiding places. There was no need for underground lairs when the entire earth was free of sunlight.

"This is good news. That means there must be multiple access points," Meghan said. "That trapdoor was probably an emergency escape hatch."

"That's what I was thinking." Werewolves weren't the only creatures that would've threatened vampires in desolate areas. They would've needed a quick escape route. Vampires were nimble. They could've dropped to the tunnel floor and landed upright. They had their flaws, but they were a far more graceful species than witches and werewolves.

We continued along the tunnel in silence. Although I'd ventured into many tunnels in New York City, this underground network seemed different somehow. I had a sudden memory of Olis beside me, using his magic to light the path. I felt a pang of grief at the thought of the wizard who'd betrayed me. I didn't know why I felt such a deep sense of loss. The wizard and I had shared a cordial, professional relationship. He'd served as my direct supervisor, yet I still found myself viewing him through the lens of father figure. I shouldn't have, really. Olis had never pretended to be anything other than my boss. And he'd been upfront about his involvement with scheming witches and wizards. He had, however, pretended to put House safety ahead of Trinity Group's interests, so there was that.

"What is it?" Meghan asked.

I shook off the mixed emotions. "Nothing."

Meghan paused to scent the air. "This way."

"What do you smell?"

"Not sure, but whatever it is, it's been here a long time."

I kept a light grip on her elbow as she progressed through the tunnel. Occasionally I reached out and let my fingers graze the wall to see whether there were more carvings. The sheer number of indentations told me these tunnels had been in use for a very long time.

"Do you think they lived down here, too?" Meghan asked.

"It makes sense there'd be a section for residences. Otherwise, they would've had to travel to the tunnels from their homes during daylight hours, which would kind of defeat the purpose."

There was no telling how far these tunnels might take us. If we weren't careful, I could end up back near the St. Lawrence River and lose all the ground I'd covered today. I didn't have time to go backward, especially in light of Renee's information. I needed to get to Connecticut, find out how to destroy the dagger, and warn Alaric before the Great Gathering.

When did he even have time to plan an event like that? Part of me was proud of him for making reform a priority. There'd been talk of synthetic blood and vaccines that made human blood unpalatable to vampires. Maybe Alaric was preparing to present his case to all the royal Houses at once. I had no idea how such a proposal would be received. I knew King Callan would be open to it. Apparently, he'd already been manufacturing synthetic blood, so he'd be ahead of the curve. House Nilsson, though. If they rejected the proposal, would that set the Houses up for a future war? I hated to think of Michael and Genevieve on the wrong side of history.

"What's this?" Meghan whispered. She held up her tiny

flame to reveal a door. It seemed out of place as there were no other doors along this stretch of tunnel.

Meghan kicked it down in one swift move.

"So much for the subtle approach," I murmured.

With a stone coffin that took center stage, the room was best described as crypt-meets-pantry. Cans and jars were packed on the shelves that lined the walls. The presence of more modern items like plastic bottles threw me for a loop. I noticed a set of rusty tools on the edge of one shelf. I felt like a time traveler, straddling multiple centuries at the same time.

"What is this place?" Meghan asked.

"An old hideout, I guess." It made sense that a vampire or two would've continued to make use of the tunnels until the Eternal Night began.

Meghan picked up a tin can from the shelf and read the label. "Green beans in a can? That's gross." She returned the item to the shelf.

I spotted a cooler on the floor and popped open the lid. Bags of blood were piled inside. I was no expert, but I couldn't imagine they'd be any good to drink now.

Meghan pushed the lid on the coffin.

"What are you doing?" I asked.

"I want to see if they left any valuables behind. Might come in handy if we need to buy weapons on the way to save your boyfriend."

I joined her at the lid as she moved it aside. We gasped in unison, startled to see a body inside.

Meghan swore loudly. "It's supposed to be empty."

I leaned forward and peered over the edge. A vampire was laid to rest inside. His eyes were closed and his arms were folded in an X. His milky skin sagged in places and patches of hair grew in random spots like in front of his ears.

Meghan loomed over him, using the lighter for a better view. "How old do you think he was?"

I scrutinized the tangled mass of silver hair. "Old."

"I bet he's been here for a long time." Meghan motioned to the shelves. "Most of these items are pre-Great Eruption."

I gazed at the vampire. "It must be so sad to die in a place like this all alone."

Two eyes popped open to stare back at me. "I most certainly did not die alone. How rude."

Meghan and I jumped backward. One of us screamed. It might've been me.

The vampire sat upright. A sharp set of fangs poked out as he stretched his jaw. "How did you get in here? Did I forget to lock the door?"

Meghan gave him a sheepish look. "I may have kicked down your door. Sorry about that."

The vampire focused on us. "You're not vampires."

"Witch and werewolf," I said, pointing in the relevant order. "What's your name?"

"Edgar." He flexed his fingers and tilted his head from side to side. "Would you mind helping me out of here? I'll be fine once I've eaten and worked out the kinks."

Once I've eaten. I cut a glance at Meghan. "Maybe waking him was a bad idea." It seemed to me that if Edgar had been asleep all this time, he was going to be very, very hungry.

The vampire seemed to grasp our distress. "No need to worry about me going feral. I've been storing supplies for years."

I nodded at the cooler. "If you mean those bags of blood, I don't think you want to drink those unless you want to be sick."

Edgar leaned over the side of the coffin to glimpse the cooler. "I'm sure the blood is perfectly edible. I have a system." His gaze slid to the shelves and he frowned. "Rusted? But how?"

"Any idea when you went to sleep down here?" I asked.

"I believe it was the year 2020. I tend to take my sabbaticals during even decades."

2020. Meghan and I exchanged looks.

"Then you don't know," Meghan said.

Edgar's brow creased. "Know what?"

"About the sun." She waited for a response. "Do you know about ten supervolcanoes going kablooey?"

Edgar blinked in confusion. "Is this a joke?"

"You missed the Great Eruption," I told him.

"The great what?" He tried to climb out of the coffin unassisted. Finally, I interceded and helped him.

"Calderas went nuts, blew monsters into existence." Meghan looked at him expectantly. "None of this rings a bell?"

"It wouldn't if he's been down here since 2020," I said.

"You've been in here so long, you missed the fact that there's an Eternal Night happening out there." Meghan motioned to nowhere in particular.

"Eternal Night? What is that?"

Oh, wow. "Long story short, the sun disappeared and vampires emerged from..." I waved a hand. "Places like this. They took over the world."

His eyebrows inched up his silver hairline. "Did we really? Good for us." He proceeded to perform calisthenics. "Is that why you're down here? Witches and werewolves have been forced into hiding? Quite a reversal of fortune, eh?"

"It isn't as though either of us was ever at the top of the

food chain," I said. "Why have you been in your coffin all this time?"

Edgar began to jog in place. He was pretty spry for a vampire who hadn't eaten in a very, very long time. I was grumpy after a day.

"I would awaken every couple decades, do a bit of rampaging, gather supplies, then retreat back here for a rest. My brother Claude..." His brow furrowed. "Have you seen Claude?"

"Just you," I said.

"That explains why I overslept this time." He rubbed the back of his head. "I suppose Claude is dead. He wouldn't have left me otherwise."

"I'm sorry for your loss," I said.

Meghan grunted. "You and I are probably the only two who'd say that to a vampire."

"I can think of a few more."

Edgar gave us a speculative look. "You don't fear my kind?"

"I was married to a vampire," Meghan told him. "And she *should* marry a vampire, but she's too stubborn."

Edgar regarded me with interest. "A vampire paramour, eh? Lucky bloodsucker."

Alaric wouldn't be lucky if I couldn't get to him in time to save him.

"I think you should eat before you faint," I told him. "What's your usual routine when you wake up?"

He glanced at the cooler. "Blood first, then a bit of food to get the teeth and gums working again." He sighed. "You really don't advise the blood bags?"

"I really don't."

"Is there a town nearby where I can feed? I could attack

you both, I suppose, but you seem nice. Besides, it'll take me days to get back to my full strength."

And based on the color of his hair, my guess was that full strength was very strong indeed.

"Vampires are a little more civilized these days when it comes to blood," I explained. "There are rules."

He laughed. "Rules? You're joking."

"House August is the royal vampire family in charge of this region. The king has been working on a couple methods that allow vampires to drink blood without harming humans or using them as a food source."

Edgar's jaw unhinged. "Is there a hidden camera somewhere? Am I being punked?" He searched around us.

"No, this is real," I said. "If you go aboveground, you'll see it's nighttime no matter what time of day it is. The cities are obviously better lit and try to imitate traditional day and night with lights and magic, but rural areas like this are mainly dark."

He shook his head in disbelief. "An eternal night. Isn't that something? I wonder if any of my old friends survived to see this."

"This network seems extensive," I said. "Would you be able to tell us how to get out of here?"

"And where we'll end up?' Meghan added. "We're kind of pressed for time."

"We need to head east, and steer clear of the local werewolf pack in the process," I told him.

He grimaced. "I'd like to steer clear of them too. Not a fan of the fur gang. No offense."

"None taken," Meghan replied. "I thought I was fitting in but turns out I was fooling myself."

Edgar's gaze flicked to her. "Been there, done that.

When you live as long as I have, you learn not to seek validation from others."

"If you say live, love, laugh, I'm shoving you back in your coffin," I warned.

Edgar coughed. "I'm parched. Where's my water?"

I located a jug on the lowest shelf and handed it to him. "We're headed to Connecticut. Any idea which direction we need to go from here?"

He held up a bony finger. "I have a map of the underground system somewhere. Let me think." He rummaged through the mess on the shelves until he found a thin pamphlet. Unfolding it, his eyes narrowed and he turned the pamphlet upside down.

"That's better."

Meghan brought the lighter closer to help him see. I tried to read over both their shoulders, but the map was faint and steeped in shadows.

"Do you have a compass?" he asked. His voice seemed to get raspier the more he spoke.

"No, we weren't exactly planning on this detour," I said.

He pointed to a spot on the map. "This is where we are. If you turn left and then right at the next intersection, you should be able to follow that for a few miles due east."

A howl echoed in the chamber, causing the hair on my arms to stand on end.

Meghan's lip curled in response. "I guess they tracked our scent."

"I don't suppose you have any weapons stashed down here," I said to Edgar.

"Afraid not, but I'm happy to hold them off and give you lead time."

Meghan and I exchanged looks of surprise. "Why would you do that?"

He rolled his neck from side to side. "Because, my dear, I'm famished."

"But you said you weren't strong enough..." I began.

He cut me off with a look. "I was being modest. Besides, I've always had a taste for wolf blood."

Meghan hesitated. "Maybe you could just drink without killing them?"

Edgar smiled, exposing his impressive fangs. "I'll see what I can do."

Another howl reverberated in the small chamber.

He gestured at the door. "Go now before you lose your lead completely."

"Thank you, Edgar."

"This is as much for me as for you." His face sharpened. "Go!"

Meghan and I bolted from the room and turned left. Edgar stepped into the corridor behind us and faced the other way. Although I couldn't see anything past him, I felt the vibrations from the wolves' thundering steps.

"Ride on my back," Meghan insisted. Before I could protest, she shifted. There was no point in arguing now. Climbing on her back, I clung to her fur with a death grip and off we went.

Chapter Ten

Meghan ran until she nearly collapsed. We exited the tunnel via the base of an oak tree, which dumped us on a forgotten road that ran parallel to the highway. She changed back to her human form and curled into a ball by the side of the road.

"Stomach cramp," she moaned.

"You ran too fast."

She gave me the stink eye. "We were running for our lives, Britt. I couldn't exactly move at a leisurely pace."

"Can I get you anything?"

"Do you have anything?"

I snorted. "No."

"I have money on me," Meghan said. "Not a lot but it might be enough to get us to the casino." She sat up and rested her head between her knees. "Why are we going to the casino again?"

"Because the magician with the Sight told me to."

"Even though there's a threat against the king's life starting tomorrow?"

I groaned. "There are multiple emergencies, okay? The

casino is on the way to New York City anyway." Maybe Roger had reached the compound by now and told Alaric about Olis's treachery.

Maybe.

The Starlight Casino seemed to be planted in the middle of a former farm. There was nothing else around for miles.

"Where do people stay when they come here?" I asked aloud.

"There are rooms in the casino."

"It must be bigger than it looks then."

"Who are we looking for in the casino?"

I laughed awkwardly. "Malcolm didn't give me a name. Only a description. Red hair and freckles."

She perked up. "Freckles? That shouldn't be too hard to find. Let's divide up and check as many faces as we can."

"Or we could just ask if anyone at the casino meets that description."

Meghan ignored my suggestion. "We could stage a fight."

"Why would we do that?"

She shrugged. "Because it's fun."

I gave a rueful shake of my head. "Is this a vampire-owned casino?"

"Aren't they all? When they say the House always wins, they aren't kidding."

If Alaric technically owned the casino, I might be able to get a message to him through the casino manager, although I still had the same issues as before. Without knowing whether Olis was still in charge of security, I couldn't risk contacting Alaric through regular channels. My best bet remained to speak to him in person.

The casino was obnoxiously loud with bright colors

flashing in every nook and cranny. It was immediate sensory overload. I blocked my ears and closed my eyes for a moment of relief.

"And here I thought Trinity Group was my biggest threat," I murmured. Starlight Casino was running a close second.

"You go left and I'll go right. We'll meet in the middle on the other side," Meghan instructed.

I threaded my way through machines, pausing to glimpse each face. Most of the players looked so miserable, I wondered why they bothered to spend time here at all. The casino needed more mirrors and fewer flashing lights. Then again, they wouldn't want to drive their customers away with a heavy dose of reality.

I had a momentary thrill when I spotted a woman from the back with bright red hair, but when I looked at her face there was nary a freckle to be seen.

A security guard seemed to notice my inspection of the customers because he meandered over to intercept me. "Can I help you find a machine, miss?"

"No, thanks. I'm looking for a friend. Red hair. Freckles. Have you anyone that fits that description?"

"Male or female?"

"Yes."

The security guard's brow furrowed. "I beg your pardon?"

I sighed. "Okay, I'll come clean. This is embarrassing, but I'm supposed to meet a blind date here. That's all I know. They could be male or female. I date both."

The security guard's gaze swept the room. "I haven't seen anybody on the floor with those features, but it sounds like Rudy DeMarco."

I resisted the urge to punch the air in triumph. "Where can I find Rudy?"

"He's on the payroll of this casino. Usually hangs out with private parties in one of the suites."

'On the payroll' was ambiguous. "Would you mind directing me to the suites?"

"Oh, you need permission to be back there."

I smiled at him. "You're on the security team. Can I get yours?"

His gaze darted left to right. "I don't know..."

I inched closer to him, continuing to smile seductively. "I'm his date. I bet he'd be real grateful to the one who directed me to his bedroom."

"Technically, it's not his bedroom," the guard stammered. "Although it does have a very nice bed. Most of the suites are luxury. King-sized bed, the works."

I dragged my nails down his forearm. "I'd love to see for myself."

Two pink spots bloomed on his cheeks. "Follow me." He spoke into a walkie talkie. "Escorting a customer to the suites. Cover Area B. Over."

A voice responded in the affirmative.

I walked alongside the guard as we passed a row of poker tables. "What else can you tell me about Rudy? Anything that might help me make a good impression?"

"He's a consultant."

"What kind?"

"Mostly he makes things disappear."

"Wizard?"

He lowered his voice. "Mafia."

I wondered whether his talents extended to making an obsidian dagger disappear.

"So, he's an assassin?" Look at that, my fake date and I already had something in common.

"Not as simple as that."

I laughed. "I can assure you, there's nothing simple about being an assassin." I cleared my throat. "Not that I would know."

The guard leaned over and whispered, "He once managed to make an entire building in Hartford disappear along with everybody living in it. Nobody knows what happened."

"He blew up the building?"

"No, he destroyed it by making it cease to exist."

We arrived at the entrance to a long corridor. There were less lights here. Less noise too.

"We're looking for Rudy DeMarco," the guard said to the colleague posted at the end of the corridor.

"Bellatrix Suite."

"Alone?"

"I believe so. Sleeping one off." His mouth curved upward at one end. "I wouldn't want to be the one to disturb him."

"She's expected," my escort said and urged me forward.

We passed the guard and two more doors before arriving at the door labeled Bellatrix Suite.

"I think I should be alone for this part," I said sweetly. I made a show of fixing my hair. It was hard to imagine the state of it considering the last time it was washed.

The guard ducked his head in embarrassment. "Yes, of course."

"Thank you for your help." I waited until he turned his back and walked away to knock gently on the door.

I heard a grunt from inside that I took as permission to enter. I stopped short at the sight of Rudy DeMarco in his boxer briefs. It wasn't every day you met a vampire with red curly hair and freckles all over his body.

"You're Rudy DeMarco?" His hair was damp and there was a crumpled towel on the edge of the bed.

He appeared unfazed by my arrival. "Sure am. With whom am I having the pleasure?"

I lost my train of thought, transfixed by his unusual appearance. "Um, my name is Britt." Did I mention the freckles? They were such a rarity in an Eternal Night world and even more of a rarity among vampires. I didn't even realize it was possible for a vampire to have them. It was likely he had another species somewhere in his bloodline, not that I'd ask him. Vampires were very touchy about their lineage. None of them wanted to be accused of having inferior DNA.

"And how did you find your way to me, Miss Britt?"

"A mutual friend recommended that I visit you for information."

He picked up the towel and rubbed his damp hair with it. "Information, huh? Our mutual friend must have mistaken me for a library."

I plastered on an agreeable smile. "I think we both know you're a vampire of many talents, Mr. DeMarco.

His gaze raked over me. "I'm getting a revenge vibe. Ex-husband problems? You need to make him disappear?"

"Not a 'him.' An 'it.'"

His bushy eyebrows inched their way up his forehead. "You've piqued my interest."

"An artifact made from obsidian. I want to destroy it."

His reddish-brown eyebrows inched up toward his hairline. "You know, most folks want to preserve artifacts, not destroy them. What's so bad about yours?"

I smiled. "It belonged to the aforementioned ex-husband. His most prized possession, in fact."

He pointed at me. "See? I told you I got a revenge vibe. Rudy's never wrong about these things." He snapped his fingers. "Lemme see this prized possession."

"I don't have it with me," I lied.

"Why not?"

"Because he has me followed everywhere I go."

Rudy scowled. "I hate guys like that. He threatening you, too?"

I rolled my eyes. "All day every day."

"Gimme his address and I'll take care of him *and* the dagger."

"You're too kind. I'm content to let him live out his miserable life. It's only the artifact I'm interested in destroying." I hesitated. "Can you tell me how to do it?"

"Lady, I haven't met a job yet I couldn't handle, but I need more details."

"It's called the Blade of Fire."

"Never heard of it."

"Does that mean you can't help?"

"'Course not. Just means I'll learn something new today, which I appreciate. I've got a word-of-the-day calendar, but I prefer real information."

I surveyed the luxury suite. "Sounds like a library would've suited you better than a casino."

He shrugged. "Family business. Couldn't have done anything else even if I'd wanted to. My sister operates out of Providence. My brother's in Boston. I even got a stable of dragons stashed in Newport."

"How do you keep dragons without anybody knowing?"

Rudy peeled back his lips. "Oh, they know. If you know

what their sweet spot is, though, you keep 'em so happy they don't flap their gums about it."

"What do you use the dragons for?"

"Anything you want. Property disputes. Revenge. Transport to a big event." He examined the gold rings that adorned his fingers. "Dragons are more versatile than people realize."

I tried to imagine a couple of teenagers arriving at their prom on the back of a dragon. If it actually happened, it didn't happen in the city.

"I don't need a dragon."

He grabbed a shirt and trousers off a hook on the door and began to dress.

"Do you want me to turn around?" I asked.

"I'm not modest."

"How is it that a family of vampires is so adept with magic?"

Rudy buttoned his pants. "You want my help or not?"

I opened my arms. "I'm still here."

"Yeah, I noticed. Not sure you'll want to pay the price for my help."

"I'll pay."

His mouth turned up at one corner. "You say that now..."

I stared at him so intently that I could see the tiny flecks of brown in his green eyes. "What's the price, Mr. DeMarco?"

"It's a sliding scale. Where's the artifact now?"

"In a safe place."

"You really don't have it with you?"

I shook my head. "Not that stupid." Okay, I was that stupid, but my options were limited.

He grinned. "You don't trust me?"

"You're fine. It's the universe I don't trust. It has a habit of conspiring against me."

He wagged a finger at me. "That sort of catastrophic thinking is a form of anxiety. You should talk to a qualified professional."

"It's only a form of anxiety when it isn't true." In this case, the world could, indeed, stop spinning on its axis.

He removed a business card from his pocket and handed it to me. "I highly recommend Dr. Valenti."

I studied the card. "Licensed in advanced mixology? Where does the 'doctor' come from?" There was no mention of a medical degree.

He ignored the question. "You'll like her. Excellent bedside manner."

I stuffed the card in my back pocket. "I have more pressing concerns at the moment but thanks."

"The mental health of the lower classes is a hot button issue. If we can improve the mental state of subjects like you through a combination of therapy, elixirs, and better living conditions, imagine what a difference that would make."

I eyed him closely. "You think it would stamp out the resistance? That if species have access to professionals like Dr. Valenti they'll decide life is good enough as it is." I barked a laugh. "You really don't get it, do you?"

He seemed genuinely perplexed. "These are all good things. Tell me. If you've got this artifact stashed in a safe place, why not leave it there instead of wasting your time trying to figure out how to destroy it? Your ex still won't have it."

"Because the only way to be certain my ex can never get it back is to make it cease to exist," I said, borrowing his phrase. "So how much will it cost?"

"Let me ask you this. What's revenge worth to you?"

I took a pen from the nearby desk and scribbled a number on a scrap of paper. I handed the paper to him.

Rudy glanced at it, his expression neutral. "You've got this on you now?"

"No, but I can get it." Once I made it to the compound. Alaric would pay.

The door burst open and Meghan appeared with the biggest smile I'd ever seen. In her hands she carried a bucket. Two security guards appeared behind her, out of breath.

"Meghan, I'm kind of in the middle of something," I said.

"But look! Money!" She shook the bucket, and I heard the sound of coins clinking together.

"Where did you get that?"

"I won it." She tossed an angry glance over her shoulder. "I won it fair and square, and you can't prove otherwise."

"You kicked the machine until it spat out all the money," one of the guards said.

Meghan slammed the door and locked it. "Those guys are a real buzzkill."

I grabbed the bucket from her and placed it on the bed in front of Rudy. "There you go. Payment in full."

"Hey!" Meghan objected.

"It's for the cause," I said through gritted teeth.

Rudy stared at the bucket of coins. "I'd have to count it first."

I jabbed a finger in his chest. "It's enough, Rudy."

"Fine. Consider it a discount because I find you interesting." He crossed the room to retrieve his suit jacket. "Who's your friend?"

"This is Meghan."

"Werewolf, huh?"

"That's right."

"You really kick a machine until it gave up the goods?"

She beamed. "I really did."

Squinting, he pointed a finger at her. "I like your style." He removed a pearlescent sphere from the inner pocket of his jacket.

"I was expecting a book," I said.

"You got something even better. I have an entire floor of books in the basement of my house, but they're a pain in the ass to access, so I hired wizards to download all the information into this orb."

As I moved to touch the orb, he clucked his tongue.

"You won't be able to use it without my authorization." Wriggling his fingers, he placed both hands evenly on the orb, which produced a faint clicking sound. "Says you'll need a diamond pickaxe."

"I've never heard of a diamond pickaxe."

He snorted with laughter. "You never heard of Minecraft, I guess."

"No, what is it? A mystical object?"

"A game. Pre-Eternal Night. Kids used to play it."

"And there was an obsidian dagger in this game?" That seemed dangerous.

Rudy shook his head. "It was a computer game. The obsidian was in blocks, and they'd use a diamond pickaxe to break it apart."

Manual labor as a game. Interesting. "Do you see anything helpful?"

The vampire licked his finger and returned his attention to the orb. "Here's something."

"You've got a lot of freckles," Meghan said, somewhat in awe.

"You should've seen him without his clothes," I said.

She shot me a quizzical look.

"It's referring us to another source," he said. "That's how research goes sometimes."

"Can you access the source on the orb?" I asked.

"Sure." He said the title and author name and waited.

"Now what?" I asked.

"Now I've accessed the resource." He passed the orb to me. "Ask your question and the orb will show you the answer. Be as specific as you can, otherwise we'll get back a bunch of irrelevant results. I don't know about you, but I don't got the time to sort through those."

I definitely did not have the time to waste. "I would like to know..."

Rudy interrupted me with the shake of his head. "Needs to be in the form of a question. No statements."

I cleared my throat and started again. "How do I destroy the Blade of Fire?"

For a moment, nothing happened. Then the orb began to glow with a soft, blue light.

Rudy angled his head to regard the orb. "Blue flame. That's what I see."

"What about a blue flame?"

"That'll destroy your dagger."

I tried to think of instances where I'd encountered a blue flame but came up empty. "I'm supposed to track down a blue flame and stick the object in to destroy it?"

Rudy chuckled. "Is anything ever simple that's worth doing?"

"Not in my experience."

"Mine neither." He returned his focus to the orb. "Not any blue flame. It's gotta be pure."

"Pure," I repeated, more to myself. "What does that mean?"

"Someone innocent. What else?" He snorted again. "Good luck finding them in this world."

"So, I need a young witch or wizard with access to advanced fire magic."

Rudy's eyes turned to slits as he studied the orb. "I'm seeing the symbol for female. That's the one with the circle and the cross below it, right? I always get them mixed up."

"Yes, that represents females."

I returned the orb to his outstretched hand. "That's it? No incantation?"

"Nope. Just a pure blue flame. Toss that sucker in and buh-bye." He released the orb. "Know where you can find any talented young witches?"

I smiled at Meghan. "As a matter of fact, I do."

Chapter Eleven

Now that I had the information I needed to destroy the dagger, I had to stop the massacre at the Great Gathering, and that meant a return to New York City. Given the time constraints, Connecticut was too far from the city to travel by foot, and I didn't have access to a vehicle. There was, however, a direct train to Grand Central Station.

"You don't have to come with me," I told Meghan. "You've done more than enough."

"No kidding. You stole the money I stole."

"It was for a worthy cause."

Grinning, she jangled her pockets. "I may have slipped a few out of the bucket before we left Rudy's suite. I'll ride the train with you to New York, then you're on your own."

"Where are you going after that?"

"I'll continue to D.C. Sounds like Twila might be able to use an extra pair of hands."

I smiled at her. "You could've stayed the last time you visited."

"I know. I just wasn't sure it was the right move."

"And now?"

"A bunch of kids running amok. No structurally sound buildings." She shrugged. "I think it's where I belong."

The moment the skyline came into view, I felt an unfamiliar pang in my chest. I didn't push away the feeling. I sat with it, examined it under the proverbial microscope like an emotional specimen.

Home.

That's what the pang told me. I was home.

I said goodbye to Meghan and disembarked from the train. A spring formed in my step as I exited the station. Alaric was mere blocks away. As much as I wanted to see him, I had to exercise patience. If I rushed to the compound, I risked capture. I had no idea how deep Olis's deception ran, nor how many members of House staff were involved. I had to take a more methodical approach. A reverse assassination, if you will.

I walked along the dimly lit street. Several lights were out. It seemed no one was monitoring this area. I made a mental note to tell Alaric when I had the chance. Infrastructure was important and House August had always excelled in that area.

This strip of the city seemed somewhat deserted. There were no pedestrians within sight. Odd, given the location and the time of day. Maybe it was the upcoming gathering. It wouldn't surprise me to learn the city had taken time off to celebrate the arrival of the other Houses. Alaric's idea was unprecedented. I was so proud of him. Gods, I hoped I had the chance to tell him in person.

A lone butterfly emerged from the shadows. The wings weren't green and gold like Alaric's but maroon and black. A single butterfly wasn't part of a patrol.

I advanced forward and cast a quick glance over my shoulder. The butterfly followed.

A shiver rocked my body. This couldn't be good.

I jumped behind a royal mailbox as the butterfly exploded into a substantial figure. Broad shoulders. Muscular arms so long that his knuckles threatened to graze the sidewalk.

I sprinted away—well, I tried. One of those long arms snatched me by the scruff of the neck and dragged me backward. The vampire was strong.

But I was smart—and I'd choose brain over brawn any day of the week.

"You came back to New York." He made a guttural sound. "That's twenty bucks I'll never see again."

I stopped resisting and spun around to face him. "You bet on me?"

"Not just me. A few of us in the Assassins Guild. I bet twenty that you wouldn't be stupid enough to set foot back in the city." He gave a rueful shake of his head. "Lesson learned."

"You say stupidity. I say bravery."

He started to roll up his sleeves with methodical precision, revealing a set of powerful forearms. "At least I'm the one who'll get the bounty."

"Who put a bounty on my head?" No self-respecting member of Trinity Group would hire a vampire assassin, and they certainly wouldn't be able to submit a job with the Assassins Guild.

He smirked. "Wouldn't you like to know."

"I would. That's why I asked. I need to know where to lodge my complaint when I leave you."

Laughter boomed. "You're not leaving here, Blood Witch. Not now. Not ever."

"What's your name?"

"Chester."

I rolled my eyes. "There's no way on God's not-so-green earth that I'm going to meet my death at the hands of someone named Chester. Sorry. Not happening."

He stiffened. "There's no need to be bitchy. I was named after the county where my father was born. It's a nice place."

"I know where it is." Chester wasn't far from Lancaster County. "No offense, but 'nice' is a bit of a stretch. It's nothing but abandoned farms and potholes that were never fixed by the humans when they fled."

His face hardened. "You know, I was planning on a merciful kill, but now I'm having second thoughts."

I studied the vampire's stocky build. His muscular body suggested slow, languid movements. "What's your plan? Neck snap?" He'd have to catch me first.

Chester cracked his knuckles. "I was thinking of going for the artery."

I winced. "Oomph. Unpleasant and messy."

"I know, but it gives me a legal excuse to taste blood in the line of duty, plus a bit of poetic justice given your specialty." He grinned. "And I'm thinking your blood will taste exspecially good." He rubbed his stomach. "Go down nice and easy."

I frowned. "Did you just say exspecially? You know it's especially, right? No 'x' sound."

Now it was Chester's turn to frown. "It's exspecially. Like expectant or experience."

"No, it isn't." I took advantage of his momentary distraction and focused on the blood pumping through his veins.

There you are.

His eyes widened when he felt the tendrils of magic

slither through his body. "Stop! Whatever you're doing, just stop."

I tilted my head. "Make me."

His cheek muscle pulsed, and I sensed the rage brewing within. "Let...me...go."

"Sorry. It's you or me, and I didn't make it this far to choose you, Chester Polyester."

"Very mature," he ground out.

Somehow, he managed to overcome my magical hold. His arm lashed out and he knocked me to the side, breaking the connection.

"I remember you, you know."

"From where?" I didn't recognize him and those were two arms I'd never forget.

"I used to work in the dungeons at the compound, but they decided I was too violent for that job. Ended up at the Guild."

"Who's they? Olis?" Olis couldn't have hired this clown to kill me. The wizard wanted me alive.

His smile revealed a set of razor-sharp fangs. "Doesn't matter. If I hadn't been fired, I wouldn't have discovered my true calling."

"You think killing is your true calling?"

He glanced at the nearby mailbox. "I consider myself a death deliveryman."

"How clever. Who hired you?"

"That again? Did you tell your victims who hired you before you killed them?"

"No. There usually wasn't an opportunity for chitchat, but since you seem a little slow..."

The vampire snarled. "Do you think I would come to kill you without knowing your strengths and weaknesses?"

"I have no idea. I was a conscientious assassin, but you

could take the lazy approach. Throw spaghetti at the wall and see if it kills me."

The downward slant of his mouth told me he wasn't amused. "I spent money on an enchantment expressly for this assignment."

I clapped my hands. "Ooh, I love enchantments. What does it do?"

"I already showed you. You tried to slow my blood and I stopped you." He advanced toward me, and I tried to connect with his blood again. No surprise I hit a wall this time.

I withdrew a throwing knife. "Did your research tell you I'm just as skilled with a blade?"

The vampire unsheathed a larger sword. "As a matter of fact, it did."

Okay, I'd been in worse positions. One prepared vampire wouldn't be enough to defeat me.

He lunged forward. I jumped back and watched as the blade sliced through the air a millimeter from my stomach.

"Who hired you?" I asked again.

"That's confidential."

"Ah, yes. The assassin's honor code. What does it matter if you tell me? I'll be dead soon anyway, right?"

His fangs elongated and tossed his sword aside. "That's very true." He hurled himself at me. His arms and legs splayed my own and he pinned me to the pavement.

I jammed a knee into his groin and wriggled out from under him. If I could find where he'd hidden the enchantment, I'd be able to use my magic.

Chester was still in the fetal position when I scrambled to my feet. "Let me guess. You hid the enchantment next to the family jewels, didn't you?"

He groaned.

"Was it spiky?" I didn't wait for an answer. I smashed the heel of my foot under his chin and reformed my connection with his blood. The enchanted object must've shattered because I had no trouble this time. "Who put the hit on me?"

He stared at me in silence.

"Come on, Chester. We're old friends now. You can tell me." I eased up on the pressure.

"The queen," he croaked.

The queen? "Which queen?"

He sneered. "There's only one true queen."

For a vampire in New York, that was Queen Dionne of House August.

All the air seemed to escape my lungs. "You're lying."

Why would the queen want me dead? She'd never had any desire to rule or participate in House politics, which was why she passed the throne to Alaric after King Maxwell's death. Her interests were elsewhere.

"No reason to lie."

"Why?" I lifted my foot as the blood drained from his face. "Did she give a reason?"

Chester rubbed his neck but remained on the ground. "She heard you can bring back the sun. She may not want to rule, but she doesn't want to be forced underground either. No vampire does."

"You know I have to be sacrificed in order for it to work, right? Do you really think I'd let that happen?"

"Can't happen if I kill you first." He grabbed my leg and tried to pull me down.

Nice try.

I quickly gained the upper hand and pressed the sharp blade of my knife against his flesh. "I won't kill you."

"Why not?"

"Because I've turned a new leaf and I won't let you unturn it."

"You mock me for exspecially but you can say 'unturn?'" He grunted his disapproval.

"I think I'm calling the shots now, grammatical and otherwise." I let my magic seep deeper into his blood until his eyes began to close.

"But I'll kill you," he said slowly.

I smiled. "No, you won't." I removed the knife from his neck and sheathed it. "Don't worry, Chester. I won't tell anybody about our meet-and-greet. It'll be our little secret." I pretended to lock my lips and throw away the key.

"There's still a price on your head," he said, yawning. "Anybody who sees you is going to take a stab at you."

I shrugged. "Then I guess I have to make sure nobody sees me."

Which gave me an idea.

I wiped the sweat from my face, still reeling from the revelation that Alaric's mother knew about the prophecy and had hired assassins to kill me. That was going to make family dinners a tad awkward.

This was bad news. If the queen was willing to murder me, there would be others. Others who wanted me dead and others willing to volunteer for the job.

Maybe I should stay away from the compound. I didn't want my presence to endanger those I cared about. On the other hand, I had to be there if I expected to stop a coup. The irony of the queen signing my death warrant while I was attempting to save her life didn't escape me.

I held out my hand. "I need your phone, Chester."

"It's a Guild-issued phone. They'll track you with it if you take it."

"I won't steal it. I just need to make a call. Then you can have it back."

Reluctantly he removed the phone from his pocket and handed it to me. That one move seemed to sap all his energy. "Satellites are working today. That's how I found you. Somebody called in from the station in Connecticut to say that they spotted you on the way here."

Turning away from him, I dialed the number for the Knights of Boudica. A prim voice answered the phone. "I'd like to speak to London, please. This is Britt and it's urgent."

"Hold, please." I listened to a scuffle in the background and what sounded like three dogs barking at once.

"Britt, you're okay?"

"For the moment." I told her about the coup.

"I'm coming. My whole banner will come."

"No, you'll get slaughtered. We can't tip our hand, and we certainly can't risk being in the same place again." I lowered my voice. "I have the dagger on me."

"Callan is there. I have to come."

I heard the note of panic in her voice. If she felt even half as much for King Callan as I felt for Alaric, then I understood her desire to fight.

"I refuse to endanger you. Stay in Britannia City. We need to be smart about this."

There was a long pause. "Promise me you'll save him," London said.

My breath nearly caught in my throat. "I promise. I'll save them all."

Chapter Twelve

My initial assumption was that Olis had squirreled away George and Liam in the depths of the compound, but the more I considered it, the more I was certain the wizard wouldn't have left them under Alaric's nose. If a vampire reported a strange bird and a werewolf in the compound, Alaric would want to know more. That meant I had to identify another hiding spot. There was always the possibility he'd killed them, which I tried not to contemplate. I didn't think Olis had it in him. Sacrificing me was different—there was a direct payoff 'for the greater good.' Killing Liam and George simply to remove them as potential obstacles didn't strike me as an Olis move.

I considered Trinity Group's hideout—the bar where they held their secret meetings—but dismissed that idea too. Olis had a soft spot for George. The wizard wouldn't have left the phoenix vulnerable to the whims of other Trinity Group members.

Which left me—nowhere.

I decided to return to my old apartment building and

search for clues there. Knowing there was a price on my head made a visit to the building riskier than it otherwise might've been, but it was my best chance at discovering what happened to Liam and George.

I walked the long blocks across the city to the apartment building. Familiar odors filled my nostrils and I longed for a good taco. I wasn't sure why streets tacos in New York City were such a scrumptious delicacy. If I survived this, I made a solemn vow to reward myself with one.

I passed no one as I entered the apartment building, which was a relief. The last thing I wanted was to be recognized. I had no idea who might be on Trinity Group's payroll. Their treachery was already more extensive than I'd realized.

A quick glimpse of the lobby told me it was unchanged and there was no sign of surveillance. I went straight to the staircase and ran up the steps. It felt like I'd been gone for years.

The corridor was quiet and empty, and the small lights that usually lined the floor weren't illuminated. I wondered whether that was intentional, although I could recall a dozen times over the past couple years when the building lost power. Could be a coincidence.

I crept past my door and continued to Liam's. As tempted as I was to peek at my apartment, I had to focus on the whereabouts of Liam and George. If I had to resort to a locator spell, I would, but that would require the services of a magic user and I didn't know which one I could trust. For all I knew, every witch and wizard in the city was now a member of Trinity Group. They were clearly on the verge of mobilizing the troops.

I paused in front of Liam's door and listened. The entire floor was eerily quiet. No voices. No movement. Granted, it was the middle of the day and most residents would be at work, but the silence was unsettling nonetheless. It was the depth of it, like being submerged in a pool of dark water where you couldn't see or hear your surroundings. The result was disorienting.

I pressed an ear to the door. Inside I heard the slightest rustle. It might be nothing—a window left open. Then again, it might be Liam, trapped inside his own apartment. It would be a clever move on the part of Olis.

I studied the door to see if I sensed a ward. I didn't want to risk setting off an alarm and alerting the wizard to my presence.

Then I heard another noise from inside. This time it was more distinctive. A thump followed by a muffled sound. Someone was definitely inside. I couldn't bring myself to knock or call his name, though. Too risky. But there was another way.

I hurried from the building and rounded the corner to the fire escape. It didn't line up with Liam's apartment, but it was close enough that I could make my way there. Of course, there was the possibility the window was also warded.

I was willing to take my chances.

My years of rooftop stakeouts was finally paying off. I climbed the fire escape and shimmied across the side of the building until I reached his window. It was closed but unlocked. Balancing carefully, I pushed up the window and climbed inside.

The living room and kitchen appeared normal enough. No overturned furniture or strange smells. I continued to the closed bedroom door. The bed was unmade and the sheets a tangled mess. That tracked.

Then I noticed the bathroom door. It was also closed.

That did not track.

Liam had a habit of leaving the bathroom door open even when he was using the toilet or the shower.

Steeling myself for what I might find, I turned the knob and opened the door.

Liam was gagged and strapped to the toilet. In the bathtub beside him was a large cage with George trapped inside.

"Gods above." I rushed forward and ripped the gag from the werewolf's mouth.

"They couldn't strap me to the sofa?" Liam lamented. "The indignity of it all, I swear."

"Couldn't you shift and break free?"

He inclined his head toward the bindings. "Enchanted."

They might have kept him from shifting, but they weren't impervious to a good, old-fashioned blade. I withdrew my knife and set to work.

"Olis, I presume."

"Yeah. What took you so long to figure out I was missing?"

I stared at him. "When did he come for you?"

"Right after Central Park."

I groaned. "I thought he might've waited until you figured out I was missing, but he got ahead of it."

"Wait. *You've* been missing?"

"Did you think I'd leave George behind voluntarily?" I turned to greet my faithful phoenix companion. "How are you, buddy?"

"It's a fireproof cage," Liam said. "If he blew any more flames in there, he was in danger of barbecuing himself."

"You wouldn't do that, would you?" I wiggled a finger at him. "Who's such a good boy?"

George flapped his wings, ecstatic.

"If you've been here since Central Park, how does it not reek in here?" It took more effort than usual to slice through the bindings, but I finally managed to work through them all.

Liam rubbed his wrists. "We've had regular visitors."

"The same ones?"

He shook his head. "Different each time. I couldn't figure out their goal."

"They were sidelining you to buy themselves time. They didn't want you to sound the alarm that I was gone." But without the dagger and the third witch, it would've taken far too long. Liam and George would've died here eventually.

Liam regarded the cage. "Poor guy. He's been so depressed in there."

I studied the lock. "Any idea where they keep the key?"

Liam stretched his neck. "No. Never saw it. I was unconscious when they locked us in here."

I patted the cage. "Don't worry, buddy. I'm getting you out of here."

"Where were they holding you?" Liam asked.

"Lancaster. Long story." I debated whether to drop the cage from a great height and smash it open. Probably not the smartest plan. "Do you think you could shift now and break this cage?"

Liam grimaced. "As much as I'd love to channel some rage, I don't have the energy yet. I need food."

I figured as much. I offered George an encouraging smile. "Hold on a little longer, okay?"

"We can't linger," Liam warned. "They haven't checked on us yet today."

"Okay, let's get you fed and then we'll free George."

"I think they've been stocking the fridge," Liam said as

he vacated the bathroom. "They've been giving us just enough to keep us alive."

Anger bubbled to the surface. My friends had been made to suffer because of me. Olis was going to regret his choices.

"I'll be right back, okay?" I told George. The phoenix wore a mournful expression that tugged at my heartstrings.

Leaving the doors open, I followed Liam to the kitchen while he raided the refrigerator.

"There isn't much here, but it'll be enough to take the edge off and boost my energy," he said.

"Grab food for George, too." I scanned the interior of the apartment. "Do you keep any tools here we might be able to use to open the cage? A power saw?"

Liam guzzled a glass of water. "I don't want to make a lot of noise. Give me a few minutes. I don't need to be at full strength to bend two of those bars."

"What was the noise I heard earlier? It was some kind of thump and then a muffled sound."

His cheeks reddened. "I banged the side of my knee on the sink and may have let loose a few expletives."

"Well, you might want to kiss that sink because if I hadn't heard you, I might have decided to keep looking."

Liam tore into a container of noodles. "I don't even care if these are cold. I was ready to gnaw on my own arm."

"I bet."

"I probably shouldn't say this out loud, but even George was looking a little tender and juicy."

I leveled him with a look. "You're right. You definitely shouldn't say that out loud."

I heard a cry of protest from the bathroom. Apparently, George agreed with me.

"What did those bastards want to do with you in Lancaster?"

"Burn me at the stake, along with London Hayes, one of the Knights of Boudica."

He frowned as he chewed. "They didn't see the irony in that?"

"That's what I said!" I sat on the counter. "We escaped when a group of vampire assassins raided the village."

He balked. "Say what now?"

"Vampire assassins. They killed...I don't know how many. London and I escaped, along with a young witch named Talia." I gave him the abbreviated story, including the imminent attack on the compound and the assassin that greeted me outside Grand Central Station.

Liam scratched his neck. "Just so I'm clear on this part, you weren't going to leave the city?"

"No, I'd changed my mind and decided to stay. The fact that I hadn't told anyone worked in Olis's favor."

"But he knew if anybody saw George, they'd realize something happened to you."

I nodded. "I guess they decided George was a liability if they sent him with me."

"Why not kill him?" He glanced in the direction of the bathroom. "No offense, buddy."

"I'm sure it was discussed as an option. I suspect Olis couldn't bring himself to issue the order. George is a rare breed. I bet he thinks that killing a phoenix would bring bad luck. Curse the ritual or something."

"Superstition saved him." Liam cracked his knuckles. "Okay, let's move. I'm ready to liberate George."

"I can help." Although I wasn't werewolf strong, I could hold my own.

"Probably best if you stay out of the way so I don't catch

you in the chin with an elbow. There's not a lot of room to work in there."

I watched from the bedroom outside the doorway as Liam pulled apart two bars and set the phoenix free. George brushed his wing against Liam's cheek and then flew to me to offer the same greeting.

I kissed his feathered head. "I'm so glad you're safe."

"What's the plan for stopping the coup?" Liam asked. "I want to help."

"Absolutely not. You've been through enough."

He gave me an incredulous look. "And you haven't? Britt, this isn't your own personal crusade."

"I know that, but I can't let you risk your life again. You're weak as it is."

He motioned to the open cage. "Yeah, real weak."

"You know what I mean. This will be a battle, Liam."

He returned to the kitchen to suck down more noodles. "There's something I don't get. Who sent the vampire assassins?"

I chewed my lip, debating whether to tell him.

"Whoever it was knew where you were, why you were there, and that Trinity Group took you." He continued talking as he chewed. "And they had the means to send multiple teams of assassins."

"It was Queen Dionne."

Liam blew out a breath. "You can't be serious."

"I'm sure Alaric doesn't know anything," I said. "Not about me, or Olis. None of it. He thinks this Great Gathering is an unprecedented event."

"Well, he's right. It's just going to be an unprecedented event for the wrong reason."

"Roger was on his way here to tell Alaric about Olis, but I don't know whether he made it."

"I almost hope he didn't. You don't want to be a vampire anywhere near the compound this week." He checked the clock on the wall. "The welcome ceremony starts in a few hours. It's a gala." He shrugged. "I heard some of the minions chatting amongst themselves."

I looked down at the state of my clothes. "I can't go there like this."

"Obviously. At the very least you need a shower first. Your hair..."

I shot him a bemused look. "No, I mean I need a disguise. If anybody recognizes me, it's game over."

He wolfed down another container of food. "Right. Makes sense. What about that witch at The Tremont? The one they call the Fairy Godmother. Do you think she's still in business?"

Sasha. I'd forgotten about her. "Good idea. I'm not sure, but it'll be easy enough to check."

"You'll need a form of payment. Got anything?"

"I'll come up with something."

"What about us? As soon as the next patrol comes through, they'll know we got out."

"But they won't know I'm the one who did it." And they also wouldn't know where Liam and George had gone. If they expended resources trying to find them, it would be a helpful diversion.

"I know a place you can hide until this is over."

"There are a lot of assumptions packed into that sentence," Liam commented.

I ignored his pessimism. "I'll show you the way. Nobody will think to look for you there."

He swallowed another gulp of water. "And where is there?"

"The Hudson settlement."

Droplets of water sprayed my face as he choked. "You think humans are going to agree to hide a werewolf and a phoenix? Those people are down there for a reason. They don't want to interact with the world up here."

"They'll do it for me." At least I knew one family that would. And Scout would be great with George, I knew it in my gut. "You'll wait there. When the coast is clear, I'll come for you."

He shrugged. "Another day, another prison."

I glanced at the bathroom. "I hate to ask, but do you think I have time to shower?"

He waved a hand in front of his nose. "I think it's imperative that you shower if you expect the vampires not to recognize your scent. No offense but you're potent right now. That being said, we should probably hurry if we want to dodge my next welfare check."

"Fair enough. Let's get you two underground and I'll get cleaned up afterward." I'd work up a sweat in the meantime anyway.

Liam and I left the building with hoods covering our faces. George was more difficult to hide, so I gave him directions to the tunnel entrance and told him to meet us there.

"Are you sure we should split up?" Liam asked.

I thought of London. "Sometimes it's the only option."

I noticed a butterfly patrol as we made our way to the tunnels. Nobody seemed to pay us any attention.

"I can feel the excitement in the air," Liam said. "Can't you?"

The Great Gathering buzz had taken hold of the city. There were flags of other Houses on display, as well as signs on every corner welcoming the royals to New York.

"Royal fever," I murmured as we descended the staircase. There was nobody around and I was relieved when I spotted George hovering in a darkened corner.

"I'm having second thoughts," Liam said.

"Too late. We're almost there now." We'd walked miles through the tunnels. I was fortunate to remember the route.

"I'm surprised we haven't run into any monsters. I thought they were fond of tunnels."

"Olis sweeps this area regularly to keep it safe." Of course, given what I now knew about the wizard, he likely had his own reasons for making such a diligent effort.

Liam edged closer to me. "Any chance we might encounter one of his teams down here?"

"I doubt it. I'm sure Olis has more important matters to attend to now." Errant monsters would have fallen to the bottom of the list.

"For what it's worth, I'm sorry about Olis. I know you were kind of fond of the guy."

I smiled. "Thanks."

"Not to call your instincts into question, but considering your track record with Olis, are you sure about leaving us with these people?"

We were about to arrive at the entrance to the Hudson settlement. Any moment we'd have a gun aimed at our heads and a demand to identify ourselves.

"I'm sure," I said.

"Stop right there and identify yourselves," a gruff voice demanded.

Right on cue.

I held my hands behind my head. "I'm Britt. These are my friends Liam and George. They're here to visit Jim, Paul, and Scout."

The guard emerged from the shadows. "You've been here before."

"I have."

His gaze slid to my companions. "Is that a baby dragon?"

"A phoenix."

He gave a nod of approval. "You're not staying?"

"I have a date."

"With a shower," Liam muttered.

I glared at him. "It's been good to see you, too." I looked at the sentry. "Please tell them these are my closest friends and I'll come for them as soon as I can."

"I haven't lost the power of speech," Liam complained.

I hugged Liam one last time and kissed the top of George's head. I felt reinvigorated knowing my friends were safe. Now I just had to do the same for the vampire I loved.

Chapter Thirteen

The Tremont was a swanky hotel downtown. The Art Deco building survived the Great Eruption. Once a luxury residential apartment building, it seemed to be thriving in the hands of its proprietor, Sasha St. Simon.

I'd first heard about Sasha during my time as an indentured servant. A witch with the power to transform her clients into whatever they wanted. A type of shapeshifting magic that worked on others but not on herself. An illegal use of magic, of course, but vampires looked the other way as they sometimes did, especially when they stood to benefit from it. Sasha had enough internal support that I couldn't touch her even as a member of the security team.

A bellhop opened the door, and I strode through to the lobby. The ornate flooring had a slightly dizzying effect. A lone woman stood behind the counter. She wore a pale pink dress and more jewelry than I'd ever seen on one person. Multiple necklaces. Earrings that lined both earlobes. Dozens of bracelets dangled from both wrists. They clinked together as she moved.

As I approached the counter, I realized the woman towered over me.

Her bright pink lips parted. "Welcome to The Tremont. How many nights will you be staying with us?"

"I'm not here for a room."

Her gaze raked over me. "I see. How's the weather today? I haven't been outside."

I struggled to remember the appropriate response and hoped I was right. "Cloudy with a chance of meatballs."

Her smile stretched across her painted face. "That's a very old password, but I'll accept it. Won't you step into my office?" She motioned to a doorway behind the counter.

"First I need you to answer a question for me."

She cast a critical eye over me. "In my office," she said firmly.

I ignored her. "Are you familiar with Trinity Group?"

Her lip curled. "Is that why you're here? Because I already told them I'm not a joiner. I don't care what kind of power they offer me. Tell your people I'm not interested and not to come here again."

Relief flooded my system. "I'm not here to ask you to join them. I only wanted to be certain you weren't working with them."

She scoffed. "Absolutely not. It's my personal policy not to involve myself with zealots."

I skirted the counter and joined her in the office. The room was as glamorous as the lobby with a gold and white color scheme and a large gilded mirror on the wall.

Sasha gestured for me to sit.

"I'll stand, thanks. It feels good to stretch my legs."

"Then I'll join you." She rested her backside against the edge of the desk. "How can I help you, Miss...?"

"Britt."

"No last name, Britt?"

"None that I care to claim. I need a disguise."

"What you need is a good scrub. When's the last time you showered?"

"I'll shower in one of your rooms if you'll let me." It felt strange as a former assassin to be in need of magic to hide me. I'd spent years in stealth mode, but this was a different sort of secrecy.

Sasha assessed me. "What's the occasion, lemon cake? A birthday surprise? A vampires-only club?"

"Something like that. I need to enter the House August compound for a gala, and I can't have anyone there recognize me."

"You want me to help you infiltrate a royal event?" She clucked her tongue. "Strudel, I'm as rebellious as they come, but I'm not going to risk life and license so you can play assassin." Her eyes rounded. "Wait a second. You said your name is Britt." She sucked in a breath. "Listen, I don't know who recommended you..."

"Relax. I'm not going to assassinate them. I'm going to save them. The gala will kick off the Great Gathering. There will be royals from other Houses in attendance. There's a credible threat against their lives and I intend to put a stop to it."

She did a double-take. "Let me get this straight. You're a witch, a former assassin of vampires and indentured servant to the House, who wants to *save* a room full of royal vampires from being slaughtered? It seems to me you'd want to sit back and watch this play out."

"I have my reasons."

She wagged a finger. "Hold up, cinnamon bun. Aren't you also the witch who had an affair with our very own House August vampire?"

"This isn't only about the king. The group that's planning this massacre isn't the regime we want to replace vampires."

"The devil we know, right?"

"As it happens, I know both devils."

"And you'd still choose vampires? Interesting." Leaning back, she splayed her hands on the desk behind her. "Tell me more about this disguise."

"Really?" I expected her to argue or refuse me service. "You don't want to stop me?" I probably should've determined that before I spilled my secret.

Sasha splayed a hand against her chest. "Me? Hell no. I love vampires. Some of my best friends are vampires. Plus, they're good for business. For what it's worth, eighty percent of my repeat customers are vampires."

"So, you have a vested interest. Good. I'm glad we're on the same page."

"Tell me, though. What's so bad about the alternative?"

"Like you, I'm not a fan of zealots."

"You wouldn't rather have your own kind in charge?"

"Not when they kidnap me and want to sacrifice me."

She snorted. "Fair enough."

"A Trinity Group regime would result in a different type of oppression. Someone like you would certainly be out of business with magic users in charge."

"The thought has crossed my mind once or twice."

"How did you end up owning a place like this anyway?" A swanky hotel was more likely to end up in the hands of vampires. While witches weren't prohibited from owning commercial property, it wasn't exactly an easy road. The layers of bureaucracy involved made sure of that.

"I inherited it from an old friend."

"Vampire?"

She regarded me coolly. “As it happens, yes. His name was Larson. We spent a lot of time together until his unfortunate passing.”

“Then you understand my position.”

Sasha’s smile seemed forced. “Let me put it this way, I earned every brick of this hotel.” She seemed to collect herself. “Let’s conduct a little business, shall we? Sounds like Cinderella needs to get to the ball before midnight.”

“I’ve got an hour before it starts.”

“Plenty of time. How about I create a ring for you to wear that keeps the enchantment active while you need it?”

“No necklace?”

She blew a raspberry. “Oh, come on. You’re smarter than that. You know as well as I do that a vampire’s gaze is always drawn to the neck. No, sweetie pie. This will be a ring so delicate that no one will even notice you’re wearing it.”

“Sounds good. What’s the price?” I held up a finger. “And don’t say my voice because I’m going to need it if I intend to stop a massacre.”

“What makes you think there’s a price?” She batted her eyelashes in an effort to appear innocent. “Maybe I’m your fairy godmother.”

I wasn’t buying it. “The price, Sasha.”

“Nothing too taxing, honey bun. A drop of your blood magic will suffice.”

“Absolutely not, and stop calling me delicious baked goods. You’re making me hungry.” I ignored the pangs of hunger that her remarks inspired.

Sasha folded her arms. “I’m afraid that’s the price. Deal or no deal?”

I studied her. “What do you intend to do with it?”

"Does it matter? You get what you want, and I get what I want."

"It matters," I said firmly.

"Whatever my intentions are, don't you think they're worth saving your precious king and his friends?"

"My blood magic is dangerous and deadly."

She arched an eyebrow. "Is that all?"

As much as I needed Sasha's magic, I wasn't willing to compromise my recently acquired principles. "I'll let you have it on the condition that you sign a contract to do no harm with it."

Her smile evaporated. "You're serious. You'd forgo the chance to save your paramour..."

"I'd find another way. I'm not trading one life for another. I've been doing that my entire life and I'm done with it. If I give in now, I'll do it again." There was always justification for bad actions if you looked hard enough.

Sasha gave me a long, lingering look. "You are not at all what I thought you'd be, sugar plum." Her lips curved in a mild smile. "Technically not a baked good."

"The clock's ticking. What will it be?"

"I'll sign your contract. Even better, I'll share my plan for your magic to put your mind at ease. I wouldn't want you preoccupied when lives are at stake." She opened a drawer and produced a sheet of paper and a pen. She read aloud as she wrote. "I, Sasha Eleanor St. Simon, being of sound mind and body, do hereby swear under oath that I will do no harm with the blood magic of one Britt..." She glanced up at me. "Last name?"

"The Blood Witch will do."

She continued scribbling. "Britt the Blood Witch. I will use the aforementioned magic only in the described manner: to treat the condition of hemophilia of one Miss Cordelia Dunston."

All the air seemed to vacate my lungs in a single whoosh. Sasha planned to use my magic to save a life, not to take one.

She looked at me. "I told you your magic was more than dangerous and deadly. I'm surprised you haven't figured that out yet."

The realization that my blood magic could be used to help and heal rather than hurt and kill—it shamed me. My whole life I'd wielded that magic as a weapon and told myself it was my only option. But it wasn't.

It never was.

I chose that path. I took the first step and the second. And I never looked back.

"What's the matter, muffin? Oops." She plastered her hand over her mouth. "What's the matter, Britt? Not the answer you were expecting?"

"No."

"Why do you seem disappointed?"

I let the shame settle and dissolve before I answered. "I'm disappointed in myself, not you." But I could be better. I could *do* better. And I was working on it, one decision at a time.

Sasha signed the document and passed it to me, along with a pen. "I wouldn't want your voice, by the way. I sing like a siren. I have to be careful not to sing with the windows open or I risk luring unsuspecting listeners to my hotel."

I signed the document. "Sounds like a good way to drum up business."

"Oh, I'm not hurting for business, and this one is invite only, as I think you discovered." Sasha winked. "First, your end of the bargain." She held up a pin and I offered my finger for her to prick. She couldn't simply access my magic from the blood itself, so she added the necessary incantation to bind them together. She placed the drop of blood in a small jar and twisted the lid.

"I hope it works for you," I said. "Will you let me know?"

"If you manage to live through tonight, sure." She wiped her hands on the sides of her dress. "Now for your transformation. Are we thinking fairy tale princess or Mulan?"

"How about a combo? As long as I'm not recognizable and wearing clothes I can fight in, I'll be good."

"As you wish. Let me see your hand." Inspecting my fingers, she turned my hand to one side and then the other. "You're a solid eight."

"Alaric would disagree."

She cracked a smile. "I'm talking about your ring size, dumpling."

Sasha opened a long, slim drawer directly beneath the table and retrieved a delicate silver band. Then she turned to the adjacent table and removed a small purple stone from a selection. I watched with interest as she put on protective eyewear and melded the two objects together while singing an incantation. She wasn't kidding about her voice. It had a soulful, haunting quality to it.

Once the ring was ready, she slipped it on my finger. "I want you to picture yourself in your mind's eye. Imagine yourself as the warrior princess you want to be at the gala. Magic will take care of the rest."

"Thank you, Sasha. You have no idea how grateful I am to have found you."

"That's what all my customers say."

I touched the ring and concentrated on my desired image. "How do I look?"

"See for yourself." Sasha directed me to a full-length mirror affixed to the wall. I pivoted to see a raven-haired vampire in a fiery red pantsuit laden with gold embroidery. The black flats were strappy enough to pass off as formal-wear but easy enough to run in.

I inspected my face. This nose was longer and straighter, and my eyes were closer together. The biggest change, of course, was the set of sharp fangs that made it slightly more awkward to talk.

"You'll get used to the fangs. Talk to yourself for the next two hours. That will help," Sasha advised.

"It would be nice to have backup." Thanks to London, I'd grown accustomed to working as part of a team and discovered that I actually liked it.

Sasha bit her lip. "I wish I could say I wasn't worried for you."

I gave her a sad smile. "Thanks. The truth is, I'm worried for me, too." But I'd do anything for Alaric, and I knew if our positions were reversed, he'd do the same for me. If I were going to sacrifice myself, I couldn't think of a worthier cause.

Chapter Fourteen

No surprise that layers of security surrounded the compound. Butterfly patrols flew overhead to keep watch for aerial or rooftop attacks. It seemed like the whole city had turned out to observe the esteemed guests as they entered the compound. I heard shrieks of delight as prominent figures walked the red carpet to the entrance.

"King Callan, marry me!"

Fat chance, lady. His heart was most definitely taken.

I stepped in line behind a couple dressed in gemstone-colored silks. The woman's skirt was layered with purples and blues and brilliant pinks. Her brown hair was styled like a French noblewoman from the sixteenth century. A single streak of white was visible at the back. She turned to give me an appraising look and faced forward again without a word.

Don't mind me. I'm nothing special. Just here to save your jeweled ass.

I nearly burst into tears at the sight of Alaric in the receiving line. He was so close, and yet I couldn't reveal myself if I expected this ruse to work. Still, I couldn't stop staring at him as the procession line inched forward. Gods, I swore he never looked better. He was more regal. More comfortable in his role as king. I watched as he greeted each guest, shaking hands and kissing cheeks. What I wouldn't give for his kiss right now. If nothing else, I could test Sasha's magic.

A lump formed in my throat when I spotted Michael and Genevieve enter the ballroom. The young royals of House Nilsson were dressed in matching formalwear in their House colors. Good. More allies. I needed every single one I could get.

Finally, it was my turn to meet the king. Only when I instinctively bowed did I realize the kisses were reserved for vampires of nobility.

"Welcome to New York," he said.

I absorbed the sound of his voice like it was an elixir for my soul. "Thank you, Your Majesty."

"And you are?"

At least I'd had the presence of mind to concoct a story beforehand because my mind was otherwise blank now. "Charlotte, daughter of Lord Bamberg."

"Ah, House Nilsson. I'm sorry your father couldn't make it. Please let him know he was missed."

Alaric had done his homework. I was impressed.

"I certainly will, Your Majesty."

I wanted to continue the conversation if only to remain close to him, but I knew it was too risky. If my plan was successful, there'd be ample time to spend with him later in my true form.

I wandered to the perimeter of the room to get the lay of the land and scanned the crowd for any sign of Olis or members of Trinity Group. Although I was relieved not to see anyone, I knew it was only a matter of time before someone showed their face—if not at the gala, then another time over the next two days.

"Security looks tight," I remarked to the guard beside me. "My compliments to the one in charge."

"That would be Calinda. She was recently promoted and, I agree, she's done an impressive job. This couldn't have been an easy task to supervise."

I nodded. "Quite the trial by fire. What happened to her predecessor?"

The vampire's gaze darted left to right. "No one's said anything, but I have it on good authority that he disappeared without a word."

"Of his own accord?"

"Don't know and no one has the courage to ask."

Well, it didn't give me all the information, but it was better than nothing. Olis was gone. Maybe Roger was able to get a message to Alaric after all. That didn't mean Olis wasn't involved in this scheme, however. It could be the reason he disappeared beforehand, although it made more sense to have a leader on the inside to pull strings. Then again, Olis knew the compound's strengths and weaknesses better than anyone. If Trinity Group wanted to orchestrate a security breach from the outside, Olis was the best person for the job. He could've knocked over the first domino before exiting stage left.

From across the room, a pair of familiar eyes fixed on me. Uh oh.

The massive beast blazed a trail through the crowd in her effort to reach me. Apparently, all the magic in the world wasn't enough to fool Toodles.

I leaned over to greet the pozuzo, the larger, stronger, much scarier descendant of the striped jaguar. "It's good to see you, too, friend." I nuzzled her nose. "You're giving me away. You realize that, right?"

I felt a hand rest on my shoulder. "She wasn't the only thing to give you away."

My heart got lodged in my throat at the feel of Alaric's hand on my body.

Slowly, I straightened and turned to face the vampire king. "You knew?"

"Not at first. I figured it out."

"How?"

He smiled. "It's you, Britt. I'd know you anywhere, in any form."

"I even camouflaged my scent."

"Yes, but you didn't camouflage your essence. Your soul is still yours and I'm drawn to it like sea to surf." He advanced to kiss me, but I held him at bay.

"No one can know I'm here. Keep talking to me like any other guest."

Alaric plastered on a bored expression. "There. Better? Now tell me what's happening. Roger's here. He told me what Olis did to you."

"Did you kill him?"

"I would have if I'd found him. He must've gotten wind of your escape or Roger's arrival because he was gone by the time I tried to apprehend him." He cast me a speculative look. "Did you change your appearance in the off chance Olis was still here?"

"I wish it were that simple." I told him everything I knew to date.

"A massacre. That's more ambitious than I expected." He plucked a passing flute of sparkling blood. "Have I mentioned it's only synthetic blood being served this evening?" He took a generous sip.

"I'm proud of you."

His smile set my insides aflame. "Part of my plan with this gathering is to encourage other Houses to adopt similar measures. King Callan has some amazing ideas. Have you met him yet?"

"I'd love to, once I'm confident you won't die tonight."

Alaric maintained a casual air. "What's their play? Storm the compound? We have multiple layers of security. They wouldn't make it past the door."

Alaric was right. "That's not Olis's style anyway. It would be a subtler move."

His gaze dragged over me. "Is this what Charlotte actually looks like?"

"No idea."

"She's very pretty. Must be your beauty shining through."

"No need to flatter me. I'll rescue you regardless."

His eyes twinkled with mischief. "And I'll reward your good deed later."

"I have to admit, your rewards have kept me going while we've been apart."

"You'll have to tell me all about your adventures once the danger has passed."

Alaric sounded more confident than I currently felt. I was a one-witch army with very little intel.

"I hope I get the chance."

His bare fingers brushed against mine, setting off tremors throughout my body. "I should continue to mingle so as not to attract suspicion. Find me later."

"Count on it."

We parted ways and I tried to focus on the guests, to root out any sign of danger. I threaded my way through the throng of distinguished vampires, pausing here and there to exchange smiles. I drew the line at drinking blood, synthetic or not.

I entered one of the smaller reception rooms and was stunned to see a familiar vampire. He stood alone with a flute of fizzy blood in his hand as he admired a painting of King Maxwell on the wall. Sensing my presence, he turned to face me.

"Master Inquisitor, what an honor to see you again," I said. What was Vincent Dufresne doing here? There were no magical women and children to torment inside the compound.

He smiled hospitably. "Please, call me Vincent. Do we know each other?"

I kept my answer vague. "We met once. What brings you to New York?" Alaric wouldn't have invited him. He knew about my unfortunate encounter with the inquisitor in Virginia.

"My services were required here."

"By whom?"

"House Nilsson. There's some concern for their well-being while they're in another House's territory. They asked me to minimize any magical threats."

"Now you work as a security advisor?" I clucked my tongue.

"I can assure you I don't consider this a step down. If anything, it demonstrates their reliance on me. There isn't a royal vampire alive who doesn't desire my particular skill set." His lips curled into a cruel smile. "And no magic required."

I couldn't resist taking a verbal swing at him. "I don't think that's true. If I recall correctly, you wore an enchantment to protect yourself from magic, which is, of course, in and of itself a form of practicing magic."

He glowered at me. "How do you know that?"

"You told me." As subtly as I could, I reached for his blood and wasn't the least bit surprised when I hit a wall. He would've shored up his defenses after our last meeting. Between Meghan's brute strength and my magic, we put the vampire through the wringer.

"Did I? I must've liked you. I typically don't share such personal details about myself."

"You must be armed to the teeth for this event," I said. "I've heard rumblings of an attack."

He seemed to take a renewed interest in me. "As have I, which is why I opted for a shaman's services this time. I figured a different type of magic might work better against the current threat."

I folded my hands behind my back and tried to maintain a casual air. "You see the hypocrisy of your actions, though, don't you?"

He lifted his chin, indignant. "I have special dispensation in the performance of my official duties. I'm not undermining the authority of the House like these substandard creatures."

Substandard? How I longed to push his head straight through the painting.

Instead, I flashed an encouraging smile. "Admit it, Vincent. You would use magic for personal reasons if you thought you could get away with it. In fact, I'd bet money you have. All those towns you've raided to interrogate witches and wizards. You probably saw more than a few you coveted. An elixir here. A charm there." I shrugged. "No one would be the wiser."

He scoffed. "I would never risk my reputation for a few measly charms. I am the Master Inquisitor. My role is too important to the Houses."

"If you're here because of a security threat, then why are you spending time alone admiring paintings?"

"You're very combative." He sipped his fizzy blood. "As it happens, I just completed a sweep of the rooms and I've allowed myself a moment of quiet contemplation, which you interrupted."

"Are you working with Calinda?"

"I am. She's handling the exterior and I'm handling the interior. The only level I was unable to access is the dungeons, but Calinda assures me there are an ample number of guards down there and no access points from the outside."

"Sounds like you have your work cut out for you. Good luck with it." *And maybe choke on the charcuterie while you're at it.*

It was only as I exited the room that his words settled at the bottom of my stomach.

The dungeons.

Calinda's attention would be focused on keeping the enemy out—but what if they were already in?

My heart stuttered as I raced through the compound in search of Alaric. I was annoyed with myself for not thinking of it sooner.

I found him mid-conversation with a pair of vampires in powdered wigs and heavy makeup.

"Your Majesty, a word."

He excused himself and took me by the elbow. "What is it?"

"The dungeons."

"What about them?"

"Are the wizards still in custody? The three that Olis brought back from Central Park?"

His brow furrowed. "I believe so. Why?"

At the time I'd applauded Olis for his willingness to finally arrest the explosive-happy trio. Now I was beginning to wonder whether it had been part of his plan all along. Trinity Group wasn't planning to break in and lay siege to the compound. They were planning to attack from the belly of the beast first. Weaken the vampires from the inside out.

"I think Olis's departure was intended to lull you into a false sense of security. My guess is he smuggled materials to them before he left the compound."

"And they've been biding their time until tonight?"

I nodded. The loud music and general merriment would create added confusion once the magical bombs were detonated.

"The wizards will never get out in time," Alaric pointed out. "What's their exit strategy?"

"They don't have one. They're martyrs." The best thing I could say about them is they weren't complete hypocrites. If they expected me to die a horrible death for their cause, these three were at least willing to do the same.

Alaric polished off the blood and left the empty glass on a nearby table. "I will now nonchalantly make my way to the dungeons. Care to join me, Lady Charlotte?" He paused. "Are you a lady?"

"Not by most standards. Pretend I'm about to be one of your conquests." I'd witnessed Alaric disappear from a crowd in the company of a beguiling vampire more times than I cared to count.

"Can't," he said. "Nobody would buy it."

I started to laugh but his expression stopped me. "Why not?"

He lowered his voice. "Because they know."

"Know what?"

He inched closer. "That I'm completely smitten."

I couldn't resist a smile. "Did you seriously just use the word 'smitten?'" I didn't think the term was in Alaric's vocabulary.

His gaze swept the room, and he strode toward the doorway, pointing to the wall. "That painting was acquired by my mother."

"She has excellent taste," I replied in an equally loud voice. Now wasn't the time to tell him that his mother was on the list of those who wanted me dead. "Where is your mother, by the way? I haven't seen her yet."

"She's around. I saw her speaking with a royal from House Osmond earlier."

"You really managed to get a lot of Houses to show up."

"It isn't everyone but still impressive enough to be considered a Great Gathering."

Alaric continued walking with purpose along the corridor, explaining the origins of the various works of art we passed along the way. He waved off the guards as we descended to the dungeons.

The moment we were alone, he pinned me to the wall and planted a firm kiss on my mouth. "I've missed you more than I can express," he said in a husky voice. "I'm so glad you're back."

"I never intended to leave. I'd decided to stay. I should've told you, but I didn't get the chance." I slid my fingers through the wavy hair at the nape of his neck and inhaled his familiar scent.

"I'm just glad you're safe."

"Safe is probably overstating it. Alive, yes." I ran my hands down his broad chest. As much as I wanted to enjoy a proper reunion, now wasn't the time. "We need to get to the wizards."

"I know." He stole another kiss before clasping my hand. "Let's go."

It felt so good to touch him again. I'd dreamed of this moment so many times and now that it was here...

Shouts rang out from down the hall.

We were too late.

Scarface was the first one I spotted rounding the corner. Naturally he didn't recognize me, not that it mattered. We were going to fight either way.

Alaric beat me to the punch. He bolted for the escaped prisoner and sank his fangs into the wizard's neck. I'd almost forgotten how swiftly he could deliver his brand of vampire justice.

Scarface's spirits seemed undampened by this turn of events. I heard his choking laughter as I continued around them.

"You're too late," he said.

Twenty feet past them, I encountered the second wizard, free from his cell.

I smiled. "Nice to see you again, Clifford."

As I reached for his blood, the corridor went white. Heat seared my body as it flew across the corridor and crashed into the wall.

Coughing, I forced my eyes open. Dust and debris filled the air. I had to contain the remaining wizards here. If they made it upstairs, it would be too late to stop them.

I crawled across the floor in search of Alaric. The vampire had Scarface on the floor in a headlock. Blood streaked both of their faces and I couldn't tell whether the wounds were the result of the explosion or the fight.

The trio wouldn't have much magic at their disposal in the compound. They were likely only given what they needed to complete the job. It would've been too much of a risk to hide any more than that. Most of the security team was comprised of vampires. Olis wouldn't have been able to circumvent them if he were too obvious.

"What's the plan?" Alaric demanded.

"I'll die first," Scarface rasped.

"Have it your way." I heard the snap of the wizard's neck as Alaric twisted it. The wizard's body rolled face-down on the floor. The vampire king stepped over it, his face red with rage. "We need to find them."

Clifford had used the bomb as his exit strategy. No doubt the remaining two wizards were headed upstairs with more explosives.

Alaric and I sprinted upstairs, passing dead guards along the way. As we reached the entrance to the main level, another bomb exploded. The intensity of the blast knocked me off my feet. My hand slammed into the helmet of a statue.

Guests fled toward the exits. Some transformed into butterflies in an effort to escape the crowd.

I struggled to my feet and saw Alaric already on the move. As we entered the main ballroom in search of the wizards, I noticed a rush of vampires heading toward us.

"Why have they turned back?" Alaric demanded. "Get out!"

"There are warriors outside, Your Majesty," a guard reported. "They have the compound surrounded."

"Warriors?" he repeated. "What kind of warriors? Wizards?"

"No, Your Majesty. These are huge and seem to be made of clay."

Warriors made of clay. Oh, gods.

"They're golems," I told Alaric. Those clay figures in the Lancaster barn weren't part of some massive art project.

Trinity Group had stored them there until they needed them. Until now.

"They have an army?" he queried.

I nodded. Even worse, it was an expendable one. When one clay figure gets destroyed, they'll simply replace it with another one. If only I'd known, I could've demolished them when we had the chance. Too late for that now. We'd have to figure out how to do it here and now.

"I had reports of strange movement from a butterfly patrol a few days ago." The king shook his head. "I told them to monitor the situation, but I never heard anything more about it."

"Olis," we said in unison. The wizard likely made sure the follow-up report never found its way to Alaric's desk. A parting gift.

Alaric looked at me. "What can you tell me about them?"

"Each one is about seven or eight feet tall. Clay. Enchanted so they can fight you."

"But they can't die," Alaric finished for me. "Vampires can't use fangs on them, and you can't use your magic on them either."

"Can't draw blood from a stone," I agreed.

Cries for help filled the air.

"The bombs are designed to push you toward the exits where the golems are waiting to crush anyone who leaves the building."

Alaric focused his attention on the guard. "How slow and clumsy are they?"

"Slow but not particularly clumsy, Your Majesty."

Alaric offered a crisp nod. "I want every vampire who can shift into a butterfly to do so. It's their best shot at getting out of here."

"What about invisibility? They can't stop what they can't see," I said.

"Butterflies can move out of reach. It's a safer bet."

I gripped his arm. "You, too."

"I can't issue orders if I'm in butterfly form." He turned to the guard and barked, "Go! Now."

The guard bolted from the room, and I heard his shouts as he advised everyone to change forms.

"Any idea how to defeat the golems?" Alaric asked.

"If you knock off its head, it'll simply pick it up off the ground and reattach it."

His mouth tightened into a grim smile. "Lovely. There must be a weak spot."

The walls shook, causing pieces of plaster to drift to the floor.

"If there is, we'd better find it fast." A thought occurred to me. "What's their end game?"

"To kill us all."

"And then what?" I waited only a beat before answering my own question. "They're waiting to make their entrance. Mark my words, beyond the golems will be members of Trinity Group waiting to swarm the compound and make it their own."

Alaric's eyes sparked with understanding. "We should stop fighting the golems and attack the witches and wizards behind them."

"They're probably controlling the golems. They're like giant puppets. Cut the strings and the puppets fall down."

"I'll send every available vampire. They can fly straight over the golems' heads and reform to fight the others."

"I'm going to find our third wizard and make sure he can't set off any more explosions."

Alaric grabbed me by the waist and kissed me. "Meet me by the private exit when this is over. You know the one."

I knew. "Don't die."

"Like I would let that happen," a voice interrupted.

I looked past Alaric to see Roger. "You're alive." The relief in my tone was evident, even to my ears.

"It's a mess out there. When I didn't see you, I decided to come back and search."

"I'll tell you the plan on the way out," Alaric said. "Let's go."

Roger noticed my stillness. "You're not coming?"

"My fight's this way." I poked a thumb over my shoulder.

"Good luck, Britt." He and Alaric rushed toward the door.

I tried not to think about what might happen to them while I was inside. I'd never forgive myself if I wasn't there to protect Alaric from harm. I just kept reminding myself that he was a powerful vampire who could take care of himself. He wouldn't have made it this far otherwise.

I crept along the corridor on nimble feet. I sensed movement behind me and turned with a racing heart.

"Toodles," I whispered. "What are you doing here? You need to go back."

The creature stared at me in stubborn defiance.

"This way is dangerous." Who was I kidding? All the ways were dangerous. Toodles was just as likely to be killed by a golem as anybody else.

The beast moved to walk beside me. It seemed I had my own Roger.

I had a feeling the wizards weren't finished with their explosions yet. They had to keep up the pressure so that the guests felt forced to flee despite the dangers outside.

Survival would not be the third wizard's priority. I had to remember that when I found him.

I removed the enchanted ring from my finger. If this was to be my last hurrah, I wanted to be myself. At the very least make it easier for Alaric to identify my body.

I heard a scraping sound up ahead and slowed my pace. Looking at Toodles, I put a finger to my lips.

"Stop!" It was the third wizard, the one so nondescript, I never bothered to give him a nickname.

Vanilla's head snapped up and his eyes widened. "Seriously? You?"

"Yep, still alive and kicking."

His mouth twitched. "Not for long." He tried to continue the spell.

I reached for his blood with lightning speed and unleashed my magic into it. I didn't bother to use a magical scalpel. I simply flooded his blood with my magic. His eyes bugged out as his body grew rigid. The object he was holding started to slide from his hand. Despite the odds, he managed to move his stiff fingers to detonate it.

Bastard.

I lunged for the bomb as it fell to the floor.

Toodles was faster.

The beast snatched the bomb in her jaws and jerked her head to the side, throwing the device clear across the room. I dropped to the floor and covered my head as the explosion rocked the room. For a fleeting moment, I thought we'd avoided disaster.

Then the walls caved in.

The air fled my lungs as the weight of the stones crushed me. I remained on the floor and waited for my surroundings to grow calm again. Pain jabbed at me from every angle. I clenched my teeth and tried my best to ignore it. I'd tend to my wounds later. Bones could mend. Skin could be healed. As long as I could move, I could get to Alaric, even if it meant crawling across the compound floor on my stomach.

A soft whimper reached my ears.

"Toodles?"

Another whimper.

I rounded my spine and pushed the debris off my back. So far, I seemed bruised but not broken. I listened again for the whimper.

I found Toodles trapped beneath a substantial wooden beam. Her eyes fixed on me, and I saw the pain reflected in them.

"I'm going to get you to a safe place." And then hopefully find a healer once the dust settled.

It took all my reserves to move the wooden beam. I pushed it until it clattered on the floor. Then I slid underneath the creature's body so I could carry her on my back. It was difficult to breathe with so much weight on top of me, but I had to try. I owed Toodles that much.

I clawed at the heavy rocks ahead of me and used them as leverage to pull myself forward. I felt the sensation of wet scruff on my shoulder blade and realized Toodles was licking an open wound where my top had torn. I fought back tears as I continued to propel myself along the corridor.

Almost there.

Every inch of floor seemed like its own mountain to climb.

"There you are. Is this some weird bonding activity? If so, say the word and I'll leave you to it."

I craned my neck to look at Liam. With streaks of blood

across his face and torn clothing, the werewolf appeared to have endured a few injuries of his own.

"You're not supposed to be here."

"Did you think I'd let you court death without me? Friends don't let friends die alone."

"Now who's talking about a weird bonding activity?"

He chuckled. "Better late than never, though, right?" He scooped Toodles off my back and I immediately felt the difference. "Can you get up?"

"I think so. Give me a minute." I braced myself for the flood of aches and pains as I rolled to the side and pulled myself to my feet.

"I tried to persuade the humans to join us, but funnily enough, they weren't excited to defend vampire rule. I tried to argue it was the lesser of two evils, but they weren't interested."

"It isn't defending vampire rule as much as saving loved ones."

"Loved *one*, you mean."

I didn't take the bait. "Did George come with you?"

"Of course. He's outside creating a firewall."

"But the golems are made of clay."

"It isn't between the compound and the golems. It's between the golems and their masters." He examined Toodles. "She needs a healer."

"Can you get her to one?" I couldn't leave yet. Not until the fight was over.

Liam nodded. "Leave her with me."

I was grateful to my friend—and impressed that he was strong enough to carry Toodles down multiple city blocks. Next time he objected to carrying a basket of laundry, I would remind him of this moment.

The floor quaked. This time wasn't from a bomb. The stone warriors were attacking from inside the building.

"Go," I ordered.

With Toodles in his arms, Liam turned and ran.

I dragged myself through the crumbling compound to find Alaric. There was a chance he decided to join his guards beyond the golems, in which case he'd also be under threat from George's fire.

Smoke poured into the compound. It seemed every route I took subjected me to coughing fits and impaired vision. My body screamed in agony. I paid it no attention. If I gave in now, I wouldn't make it out alive. I'd come too far for that.

Death wasn't an option.

As I passed by a marble statue, I noticed someone huddled on the floor behind it. I stopped and nudged them with my boot. Slowly they turned to look at me. I recognized a vampire from the gala. His face radiated fear.

"They've come to kill us."

I extended a hand. "Come on. Let's get you out of here."

He gazed at the proffered hand with reluctance. "Are you one of them?"

"I'm a witch, but I'm not with them."

He cowered from my touch. "I don't believe you."

I sighed. There was no time for cowardice. "Can you shift?"

He shook his head. "I didn't inherit that particular trait."

"The other vampires are fighting outside. That's where I'm headed."

He remained huddled behind the statue. "I'm safer here."

"Suit yourself." It was then that I noticed the blood gushing from a gaping wound along his neck.

He wasn't a coward. He was injured and too proud to say so. A wound like that was likely fatal, even for a vampire.

"Can you walk?" There was a slight chance I could get him to a healer in time.

He averted his gaze.

That's a no then.

"Is there anyone I can contact for you? An emergency contact?"

"You...have a working phone?" he rasped.

"No, but I'll get to one eventually."

"There isn't...anyone." He tried to look at me, but the effort was too great. "Kill me," he whispered.

I swallowed the lump in my throat. For years I killed vampires without a second thought. His request should be easily granted—and yet.

"Are you sure?"

Slowly, he nodded. "Quickly."

I crouched beside him. "What's your name?"

"Alan." He tried to swallow. "Hurts to talk."

"Well, this won't hurt a bit, Alan. It'll be like going to sleep. What do you dream about?"

"Butterflies," he said without hesitation. "Always wanted to shift like my brothers."

"Then picture yourself as a butterfly," I told him. I unfurled my magic and sent it spiraling through his blood. I slowed the flow until his eyes drooped closed and his head slumped to the side. Blood cascaded down his body like a crimson waterfall.

I said a silent prayer for him and dashed to the exit.

Outside was absolute mayhem. There'd been no sign of

Alaric or anyone else inside the compound. It seemed the party had moved entirely to the city streets.

I spotted George flying overhead and my heart leaped with joy. I resisted the urge to wave. There'd be time for reconciliation later. Besides, he was focused on maintaining the fiery wall to keep the witches and wizards from their golems. I didn't want to be a distraction.

A clay foot landed beside me, narrowly missing me. I didn't wait to be noticed. I darted behind him and scanned the area. Too much chaos. Smoke burned my eyes and lungs. I could barely see the buildings around me, let alone the battling parties. I needed a better vantage point.

I turned back to the golem. If somebody was controlling this one, they seemed to have stopped. The warrior was completely still. I decided to use his paralysis to my advantage and scaled the figure's leg until I reached its outstretched arm. My body protested. Tough. I'd lick my wounds tomorrow. I swung myself onto the arm like it was a tree branch and grabbed its earlobe to pull myself onto the shoulder. Once there, I climbed to the top of its head and searched the horizon.

A cloud of dust dissolved behind us and that's when I spotted her.

Saffron. My sister.

Our gazes locked and she winced in recognition. In her hand she held a small object. Her lips moved, probably an incantation that controlled one of the golems. Beside her was another witch I recognized from the Trinity Group meeting I attended. Natasha. She, too, held a small item in her hand. I quickly identified other familiar faces from that meeting. Craig, Milton, Elroy, Theresa. It seemed I wasn't the only ace up their sleeves.

"You don't have to do this," I yelled to my sister.

Saffron ignored me. A clay arm swung and knocked me off my perch. I landed on the ground with a thud and stared up at the warrior.

"Saffron's golem, I presume."

The golem continued toward the compound. She'd only wanted to demonstrate which side she was on.

Duly noted.

I scrambled to my feet and pivoted to find her again amidst the chaos. Two vampire guards had seized her by the arms. I spotted her device crushed beneath one of their boots.

"You chose the wrong side," she screamed at me. "You should've let us sacrifice you!"

One of the guards looked across the debris at me. He squinted in recognition. "You know this one, Britt?"

"Her name is Saffron Miller. She's my sister."

She twisted and tugged to be released. "I'm nothing to you! Nothing, you whore of the Fallen!"

So much for a rebellious stage. I thought I might feel anger or resentment, but all I felt was sympathy. Saffron hadn't chosen her path any more than I'd chosen mine. We'd both been used by authority figures, albeit for different reasons.

The tide appeared to have turned. Golems were collapsing into piles of rubble. Wizards and witches were being hauled away by hordes of vampires. It was difficult to watch. I, too, desired change, but this wasn't the way, and Trinity Group certainly wasn't the right organization to take the lead.

I peered through the darkness and dust to find Alaric. As I climbed over the leg of a fallen golem, I saw him. My heart seized as I also saw a bolt of white light streaming toward him.

"Alaric!"

The vampire king ducked as the bolt streaked over his head. It would've nailed him in the face if he hadn't reacted.

I shifted my focus to his assailant and found myself face to face with Olis.

Well, it was about damn time.

I'd pictured this moment many times throughout my recent ordeal and worried that I'd hesitate if and when the opportunity ever presented itself.

My fears, it turns out, were unfounded.

I sent my magic barreling toward him. It crashed into his blood without resistance. No enchantments. The arrogance to assume he wouldn't have to fend off magical attacks.

His mistake.

I sauntered closer to him.

"Britt," the wizard croaked. "You survived. Good."

"You only think it's good so that you have the chance to kill me when it's best for your precious prophecy." I withdrew the Blade of Fire and held the tip against his cheek. "Looking for this?"

His eyes widened at the sight of the obsidian dagger. "How?"

"How do you think? True grit, you backstabbing coward." I sliced his cheek open and I felt a sense of satisfaction as blood seeped from the wound. "Too bad you'll never get to use it. I know how to destroy it. Prophecy over."

"No," he said in a horrified whisper.

I gripped his blood and used my magic as a vise, squeezing it until the flow stopped all together. His face drained of color and his jaw slackened.

Alaric jogged over to us. "Britt, stop. Let his punishment be through official channels."

I laughed bitterly. "This is war, Your Majesty, or haven't you noticed?"

"Look around you. The battle's over. We've won."

I kept my hold on Olis, unwilling to let go. I'd trusted him, but the wizard had treated me like a pawn, an object to be moved and manipulated at his command.

"Britt." Alaric's voice was softer now. "My love, I understand. Truly, I do. There are guards here who can take him into custody."

"So that he can escape? I don't think so." I kept my focus on the writhing wizard.

"You'll kill him."

"He deserves it."

Alaric placed his hand gently on my shoulder. "Britt, you're not that witch anymore, remember?"

"This is different."

"You're right. This *is* different. Before you killed for survival. This is revenge, pure and simple. That's not who you are."

Alaric was right. I'd fought too hard to better myself, to become more than a feared killer.

I released my hold on Olis and vampires rushed in to slap a pair of inhibitor cuffs on him. No more magic for the wizard. His gaze remained pinned on me as they escorted him away. I thought he might utter some sort of apology, but no such luck. Olis was only sorry that his plan had failed. I'd been nothing more than the means to an end for him. I'd put him on a pedestal, desperate for a father figure, and he'd taken advantage.

"You'll need new dungeons," I told Alaric.

"I'm aware."

I turned to face him. "Thank you."

"No, thank *you*. You saved my life. You saved us all."

I leaned my head against his chest and listened to the steady beat of his heart. The sound began to soothe the raging inferno inside me. "Can we find King Callan? London will want to know that he's safe."

"Oh, he's quite safe, I can assure you."

I straightened as another vampire made his way toward us through the rubble. His blond hair sported reddish highlights and his six-foot-five frame was toned and no doubt deadly.

"Britt, may I present King Callan of Houses Duncan and Lewis."

"Your Majesty." It was only when I attempted to bow that I realized how much pain I was in.

"No need to genuflect," King Callan said. His green eyes radiated warmth and intelligence. "London's told me all about you. She called to warn me of a possible insurrection. Said I had you to thank for the information."

"I wouldn't have made it this far without her."

He grinned. "That makes two of us."

"Is the rest of your party safe?" I asked.

He nodded. "I saw my brother, Maeron, as well as Davina. She, for one, seemed to enjoy the melee."

Of course she did. From what I'd seen during her last visit, the princess seemed to find boundless joy in battle.

"You'll stay for the rest of the gathering, won't you?" Alaric asked. "I fully intend to stick to the program."

King Callan clapped him on the shoulder. "Spoken like a true king. Absolutely. Houses Lewis and Duncan shall remain your honored guests."

He took his leave and disappeared into the compound to help the wounded.

Another royal vampire emerged from the chaos. This one I was less decidedly happy to see.

Queen Dionne's face registered shock at the sight of me. "How?"

I forced a smile. "You hired mediocre assassins, that's how."

Alaric shot me a quizzical look.

I regarded her coolly. "Would you like to tell your son, or shall I?"

The queen consort appeared at a loss. Finally, she said, "It was for the greater good, Alaric. This one has been prophesized to doom us all. Did you know that?"

"Of course I knew. It's only a prophecy, which you and I both know means very little. It isn't inevitable."

"Either way, you cannot possibly marry a witch. Your father would forbid it."

"My father is dead. Besides, Britt has made it very clear that she won't marry me."

"You've already asked her?" Queen Dionne was aghast.

I looked at Alaric. "Now might be a good time to tell you that I've had a change of heart while I've been away."

Gasping, the queen clutched her chest. "No."

Alaric stared at me like I'd offered him the world on a platter. "Are you serious or is this simply meant to upset my mother?"

"Ask me again later, when we're not in the midst of a crisis."

"Fair enough." He kissed me hurriedly and started shouting orders at the loitering guards.

"What of me?" the queen asked. "Will you throw your own mother to the wolves?"

"No, but I will restrict you to the south wing." He snapped his fingers. "Frederick and Bolton, please escort my mother to the south wing and make sure she stays there. You have my permission to use force, if necessary." He patted his mother's cheek. "You won't want to dirty your dress in this mess anyway."

She fluffed her silk skirt. "Certainly not. It's couture."

If Queen Dionne was displeased by the turn of events, she kept it to herself.

"I don't blame her," I said, once she'd been removed from the area. "I might've done the same in her very fashionable shoes."

Alaric gave me a long look. "No, you wouldn't have." He raked a hand through his hair. "Anyway, I don't intend to keep her locked away forever. I only want to remind her that she crossed a line that I won't tolerate. She wanted me to be king and now I am."

"And a damn fine one at that, Your Majesty." I kissed his cheek. "It's good to be home."

He gazed at me with intense curiosity. "Is that what this is to you? Home?"

I cupped his face in my hands. "You know what they say. Home is where the heart is."

Chapter Fifteen

"I've reached a decision," Alaric announced.

I looked up from my dinner plate in the dining hall. "Oh? And will the royal taco be chicken or beef?"

Toodles raised her head at the mention of meat. She still suffered from a slight limp but the healer expected her to make a full recovery.

"This isn't about tacos, although I like the idea of an official House August taco." He cleared his throat. "This is about the future of governance."

I set down my fork. "You now have my full attention."

"I'd like to propose the creation of the Great Council, a group that includes representatives of each species, as well as two royal vampires from the House."

"And what will this council do?"

"Enact laws. Debate topics of public importance."

My brow lifted. "Enact laws? You'd relinquish your crown?"

"As king, I'd still serve as head of the council, but we'd

have to reach a majority to take action. I, alone, won't be able to institute a rule of law."

I gazed at him in wonder. "You'd voluntarily give up your power?"

He reached over and entwined his fingers with mine. "I think we can agree that too much power concentrated in one figure is bad for everybody. Why not share it?"

"Your father might rise up from the dead to kill you just for saying that."

Alaric chuckled. "I'd like to see him try."

I shrugged. "The right necromancer. We can make it happen." I squeezed his hand and released it. "You realize other vampires might view you as weak. It could leave House August vulnerable."

"And I think it will make our House stronger than ever."

"I love the concept, but can we call it something else? I mean, we already have the Great Eruption, the Great Hall. The Great Gathering wasn't exactly a smashing success."

The hint of a smile tugged at the corners of his mouth. "Fair point. What about the United Council?"

From his perch in the corner of the room, George flapped his wings to express his approval.

"You have the phoenix vote. Please, continue."

Alaric acknowledged George's contribution and turned back to me. "Do you think Liam would be interested in acting as one of the werewolf representatives?"

"The only way to find out is to ask." I honestly didn't know how Liam would respond to the offer. Knowing him, with a joke.

"Latin will no longer be forbidden," he continued. "That should please our magic users."

I experienced a moment of stunned silence. "Do you think the other Houses will go along with you on that?"

"I can only control what happens in House August territory, but maybe this will be the first domino that fells the rest."

"Did you raise any of this to the Houses when they were here?"

"I floated it by a few trusted friends. They were receptive but noncommittal."

"It's a big deal. Vampires in the streets will be less likely to approve."

His eyes sparked with mischief. "They'll be even less thrilled to learn that I'd like to offer you one of the two seats designated for witches."

It was a tempting offer, but one I didn't feel was mine to accept. "I appreciate that you see me as someone who deserves that kind of respect."

He withdrew. "Of course you deserve it. You've fought bravely and with honor."

"But not always," I reminded him. "I can't change the past, Alaric, and there will always be those who view me as nothing more than an assassin and an indentured servant."

"Then this is a chance to show others like you that it's possible to rise above your station. If anything, your inclusion will be a symbol of change." He frowned. "Unless this is your subtle way of telling me you intend to leave again."

"No, that much I promise. I'm staying put, right here with you." I'd mistaken freedom for an open road and no commitment or obligations, when really it was the ability to make choices—and I was about to make another one. "On that note, I told you before that if you asked me again, you might get a different answer."

The vampire's smile remained intact. "I'm not sure I want to ask again. Maybe you should ask me."

"As you wish, Your Majesty." I scraped back my chair

and got down on one knee. "King Alaric of House August, would you do me the honor of becoming my husband? For better or worse. For richer or poorer."

He vacated his chair and dipped me backward. "I can think of nothing more appealing than waking up beside you each morning until the end of time."

"Wait until you hear me snore."

He pulled me to my feet and kissed me. "You don't snore. It's only a gentle wheeze. I consider it a lullaby."

I smacked his broad chest. "I also have an idea I'd like to run by you. Fair warning—it requires House funding."

"Good thing you have an 'in' with the king."

"I'd like to open an academy for young witches and wizards right here in the city. A specialized school for rare magic. There's that empty building in Hudson Square that's still in decent shape and large enough to house a school."

"Isn't that awfully close to the river?"

"The wards will be up, plus they'll have magic. They can handle themselves." And if they couldn't, they would be taught.

Alaric nodded. "Consider it done."

"I do have a suggestion for a witch representative on the council, though, if you don't object to someone from the Lancaster coven."

"No, but I'm surprised you'd recommend someone from there."

"Her name is Valentina. She has earth magic. Her magic grows the most delicious sweet potatoes you've ever tasted."

"Then by all means, we must have her on the council." He smoothed back my hair. "In all seriousness, an earth witch seems like an appropriate choice for this role. Are you certain she'd be amenable to working alongside other species, though?"

"You mean vampires?" I smiled. "I think she'd be open to collaboration. Witches aren't all cut from the same cloth, as I think you already know." I wrapped my arms around his waist. "And neither are vampires."

"Thank the gods for that." He kissed my forehead. "It's a messy life, isn't it? But still a good one."

I stood on my toes and planted a firm kiss on his lips. "A very good one."

In furtherance of my academy idea, I'd summoned Twila to New York, along with a few of her young witches. Now that Meghan was in D.C., it seemed like a good opportunity to give Twila a break.

"There's my friend," I said, as Twila entered the compound with her young charges.

Breaking into a huge smile, Talia bolted for me, throwing her arms around my waist. On a scale of Loves Warm Hugs to Don't Touch Me or I'll Skin You Alive, I landed somewhere around Approach with Caution.

"Britt, you're alive." She pressed her cheek to my abdomen and squeezed me tighter.

"Very much alive." I gave her an awkward pat on the back before extricating myself. "How's D.C.?"

She raised her chin to beam at me. "It's amazing to be with so many other kids. I never had such fun in Lancaster."

Twila ruffled the witch's hair. "She's one of us already."

"I was on kitchen duty this week. That meant I got to help with the cooking."

"And she's a natural," Twila added.

Talia seemed genuinely thrilled with her change in circumstances. It warmed my dark and twisted heart.

"What made you call us here instead of coming to the Wasteland?" Twila covered her mouth. "I really need to stop calling it that. It's far from a wasteland now."

I told her about my plans for an academy for practitioners that possess rare magic. "I'd like a place for them to feel comfortable and learn to harness their powers without fear."

A small gasp escaped Talia. "Could I be a student there?"

I stroked her head. "I was hoping you might volunteer. I'm also looking for a witch with a certain ability."

Talia's hand shot in the air. "Me. I volunteer."

I laughed. "I'm glad you're eager to help, but I need a young witch with elemental powers. Fire, specifically." I looked at Twila. "Can you think of anyone? The younger, the better."

Twila's gaze turned thoughtful. "We have about a dozen that I can think of off the top of my head. Maxine is ten. She's probably the youngest of them."

"I like Maxine," Talia interjected. "She helped me wash dishes the other day. I didn't even need to ask."

"How about someone with unusually powerful fire magic?" I asked.

Twila frowned. "Unusually powerful in what way?"

"Have you seen any of them produce white flames—or maybe even blue?" Blue reached higher temperatures than both orange and white flames, which was likely the reason that only blue fire was capable of destroying the dagger.

Twila bit her lip, deep in thought. "I can think of one I met in Richmond who can produce white. Maybe she can do blue, too."

"It needs to be a child. The youngest witch I can find."

"Ooh, is it for a ritual?" Talia asked. Excitement radiated from her.

"Sort of."

She opened her mouth to speak but then quickly closed it again.

"What is it? Do you know someone?"

She looked from Twila to me. "Me."

I laughed. "Seriously. Who is it?"

"I'm not teasing."

"But I thought your secret magic was..."

Her finger flew to her lips and she shushed me. "It is, but that's not my only one. It's just my scariest one."

I laughed. "You don't think the ability to produce a three-thousand-degree flame is scary?"

"When you put it that way..."

I studied her. "How long have you had fire powers?"

"Since I've had any magic at all."

"Is there anything else you haven't told me?"

She hesitated.

"Talia," I prodded. "I think I've shown you that you can trust me, haven't I? I can't help you if I don't know everything."

She rubbed her arms. "I've been trying to find a way to get rid of it."

"Get rid of it? Why would you want to do a thing like that?"

"Because I'm worried I'll hurt someone. Maxine accidentally burnt one of the humans with her orange flame. She was really sorry, but at least it was only a second-degree burn. If I'd done it, I would have for sure killed him."

She was afraid of her own power. This was exactly the reason I wanted to create a safe place for witches like Talia.

For witches like me.

I took her by the hand. "Listen to me, Talia. You are an even rarer witch than I realized. It's important to learn how to control *all* your abilities so they don't one day control you. Do you understand?"

Her eyes were round and solemn as she nodded.

"Would you mind demonstrating your blue flame for me? It would really help me out."

I had a strong suspicion that her father wasn't the wizard married to her mother. Talia was likely the product of an affair, which was just one more reason it was good that we got her out of Lancaster. The coven would've blamed the child for her mother's mistakes. I could think of two wizards with multiple elemental powers in the coven. It was common to have only one elemental power. Talia was already special because of her hidden magic. The fact that she possessed elemental magic on top of that was extraordinary. No wonder she was desperate to flee Lancaster. She knew how rare she was and that she'd be shunned rather than celebrated for it. Smart girl.

She blinked as she looked around the cramped room. "Here?"

"No, we'll do it somewhere safer."

"You won't tell anyone?" she whispered.

"Not without your permission, but I think you should consider confiding in others. Secrets are burdens too heavy for such delicate shoulders."

She broke into a smile. "I've been learning things. And I want to try to read your aura again."

"I thought you couldn't."

"I can't, but I've been reading about unusual auras to see if I could figure out what happened."

"London and I got under your skin, huh?" I had nothing

but admiration for this kid. She was committed to learning everything she could about her abilities. She gave me hope for future generations of magic users.

She bounced on the balls of her feet. "I want to be just like you when I grow up."

"With all those powers, you're already reminding me of London."

From the size of her smile, you would've thought I'd handed her a unicorn.

We descended to the tunnel that led to the dungeons. The area had been cleared of debris and the walls restored.

"Why are we going down here?" she whispered.

"So that we aren't in close proximity to anything that could catch fire and spread." The compound had seen enough carnage and destruction for one century.

Talia drew a deep breath. "Are you ready?"

Nodding, I withdrew the dagger.

"Ooh, that's pretty. What's it made of?"

I showed her the Blade of Fire. "Obsidian. It's a very special material and not easy to destroy."

"Why do you want to destroy something so pretty?"

"To keep me safe." To shatter the pieces on the board. To prevent a prophecy from holding my life hostage.

Talia stared at the dagger. "And if I can destroy this, you'll be safe forever?"

"Not forever," I said. "Nobody's safe forever. But it'll give me a fresh start. A clean slate."

She broke into a giddy smile. "Like me."

"Yes, like you."

"Well, you helped me, so it's only fair that I help you." She opened her hand and concentrated. I watched as a flame burst from her palm. Red, then orange and yellow, then white and finally—

Blue.

"You don't feel any heat?" I asked.

"Not on my hand. It feels nice, like holding a kitten."

If only everything felt that good.

"This is for me, for London, and the other witch I hope they never find." This was for all the pawns in the game. For all the witches who were different, and more powerful than others were comfortable with.

I placed the dagger in her hand and watched it burn.

Stories from the Midnight Empire will continue in **Golden Hood**, *Midnight Empire: New Dawn*, Book 1. You can learn more about my other books at www.annabelchase.com.

Printed in Great Britain
by Amazon